DULCE *De* LECHE

Collection of Erotic Stories

By

Monica S. Martinez

FEATURING STORIES BY:

Chante Graham
Alexandra Castillo
Tamika Peters

Poetry provided by Damyico R.

ISBN:	9780984157303
Edited by:	Brandon McCalla
Design:	Marion Designs
Photography:	Mike Pagano (www.modelmayhem.com/bigcitymodelz)

ACKNOWLEDGEMENTS

I would like to firstly thank God, with him all things are possible. My two wonderful boys God has blessed me with. You make being your mom wonderful and easy. My husband Edwin you are my strength thank you for all you do, I love you.

My mother Carmen Hamilton you are super amazing thanks for everything. Aunt Rae you are what I've dreamed about being "Super Woman." Thank you for everything you have done for me. My beautiful sisters for all of their support: Asia, thanks for protecting all of us. Raquel (Kelly) you always said that I could do anything I put my mind to. Tonii you have always been supportive in anything I came to you with. Alfie thanks for always listening to me talk about anything and everything. Brenda thanks for just being my sister. Yessenia for always letting me pull the "I'm the older sister card," Maria one of my baby sisters thank you for always giving me inspiration. Kassandra my heart, I love you for being by my side throughout my struggles.

My brother's Dimas and Al I love you. To my nephews, thank you for loving me, because, I love each and every one of you. To my beautiful nieces each and every one of you, thank you. Evelyn I must say you are awesome. You made me the woman I am today and I love you for that. I would also like to thank my ride-or-die girl Tamika you have no idea how much your friendship means to me. Thank you for supporting me and being there at any given time "all the time I love you for life." Janet my Comai you already know how grateful I am to have you in my life. Brett, my girl for life, I love you, thanks for giving me all the love and support when I needed it.

Jeannette (Nena) my marketing designer with you anything is possible. Thank you for all the other wonderful things you've done already: Catalogs, Posters, Invitations, Business Cards. My brother in law Mart Man you're the best brother-in-law ever. Well if truth be told you're the only one that has lasted in our crazy family lol. Javier thanks for supporting my goals. Khaliya, my web designer many thanks to you as well. Brandon McCalla thanks for taking care of the edits, you are simply amazing. Keith of Marion Designs my cover is hot thanks to you. Chante we got this get ready. Karen I'm so blessed to have you back in my life.

INTRODUCTION
Foreplay: provided by Damyico R.

Tonight will be the night we release all tensions

erotic pleasure is your sentence

no fantasies left unmentioned

as I explore your every inch

and your goose bumps rise

I feel your body yearning

there within your thighs

I brush your skin softly

as your nipples elevate

your nature begins to moisten

as your soft lips deviate

your mouth begins to dry as you lick your lips

in desperation

hoping not to succumb to each and every sensation

you melt into the blankets as you hold on for life your life

and my tongue explores your nature

your pelvis goes into flight

Sweat beats down your face as you ask for no more

Retracting that statement

You beg … Para mi amor

As your body explodes into numbness

and onto earth you drop, just remember one thing ma

I started at the top.

Hotel Room

Monica Martinez

The place was in Jersey, a location no one would know about. I had never visited a place like this before. This was going to be the first time; I've never cheated on my husband of fifteen years. I was scared and shaking inside but it didn't prevent me from going to meet him…

We met at a convention we both attended in New York City back in October. The laws of attraction took heed from the moment we laid eyes on each other. There he stood 5'11, 175 lbs, curly black hair which was pushed back. He had a full beard and mustache, neatly upon his boyish face. His dark eyes had me mesmerized as he looked me over from head to toe. He had riled something inside of me, which hadn't been disturbed in such a long time. I tried to avoid the feelings as I walked past him.

Damn, I was confronted once again with him on my way back from the bathroom. He extended his hand out to me "I'm Calvin," he said as I went for the handshake.

"I'm Alexis."

"Pleasure to meet you Alexis" he said placing a kiss on my hand. My pussy creamed as I pulled away. I had to get away from him. I was almost positive he knew what was happening in between my thighs.

"My pleasure Calvin but if you'll excuse me I need to get back to my booth."

We talked briefly. The lower part of my body screamed for his touch as I tried to be nonchalant and cordial, after all it was our very first meeting. I noticed the ring on his left finger. *Damn it to hell, this was gonna be harder than I thought as I saw the lust forming in his eyes.*

I felt his eyes on me as I turned my back to walk

away. Since I had his attention I walked with more *umph*. I sashayed my hips as if I were dancing salsa. I don't know what came over me at that particular moment. I turned to look one more time to make sure I had him in a trance. Sure enough he was. I smiled and waved good-bye to him. I knew it would be a matter of time before he took a break and came to my booth to talk to me.

An hour later there he was requiring my attention. My back was turned when he entered my booth, but I knew he was there. It was as if I could feel him. I turned around, our eyes locked. I looked him over with burning desire in between my thighs.

"Hey Calvin, what's up, you on a break?" I asked.

"Actually Alexis, I had to come over here and talk to you. I know you are married from the big ass ring blinging on your left hand. I'm married myself and I don't want to play games with you. You carry some serious sex appeal and you got me quiet interested. I've never cheated on my wife although temptations have been presented. Something about you has me intrigued and I know you can feel the electricity between us cuz it's quite evident."

Shit he was blunt, straight to the point. I can't say I was even offended by any means. It actually made him sexier in my eyes. *A guy after my own heart* I thought to myself. My nipples got erect and my panties filled with cream.

I smiled and said "Wow thanks for the honesty."

He asked if I ever strayed as he locked his eyes on me awaiting the answer.

I responded "No, never in fifteen years."

"Well Alexis, there is a first time for everything" he said as he handed me his business card. My booth started to get filled with potential clients. He said "Feel free and I do mean feel free to contact me at any given time. I know you feel the attraction between us. I don't want trouble but for some reason I want the kind your vibe is sending off."

I smiled for the rest of the day as I worked the convention. I past him a few more times during the day, although he was obviously just as busy as I was he always looked my way with his boyish smile. Those pearly whites looked damn tempting as I imagined running my tongue across them before sticking my tongue down his throat. He visited me one more time towards the end of the convention to make sure I was clear on what he wanted.

I was clear, shit, crystal clear.

He had me thinking after the convention as I drove home, deep in Long Island. The moment I walked inside the house, I jumped on my husband without a second thought. I fucked the living shit out of him with thoughts of Calvin on my mind. My husband of course didn't suspect a thing and welcomed the hunger from me. I closed my eyes and Calvin's face was all I saw. The cologne he wore lingered in my memory and filled my nostrils. I straddled and rode my husband with such intensity, digging my nails into his chest, an intensity he hasn't seen in a very long time. I came several times on his hard cock. His body began to tremble.

He shouted "I'm going to cum." I quickly jumped off his manhood and placed it in my mouth and fantasized Calvin feeding me with his cum. I swallowed it all without missing a drop. After an hour of pure fucking, he said "Damn baby what has gotten into you?"

I just smiled and said "Nothing, just horny I guess." He cuddled me for the remainder of the evening as I fell asleep dreaming I was in Calvin's arms.

I awoke the next morning finding myself at the computer

debating on writing Calvin. *I've never strayed why would I now?* I thought about what could be missing from my marriage, which would make me want to cheat. Nothing came to mind. I love the life we live. We are completely happy and I'd be stupid to jeopardize it for Calvin. I moved away from the computer; shutting it down convincing myself I should not contact him. The more I tried not to think about Calvin the more he came to mind.

My husband touched me the next night obviously to make love. *Shit* he wanted what I had given him the day before; the same passion. As he pulled my panties off with his teeth he playfully licked my second set of lips, I immediately closed my eyes to enjoy the sensations. Calvin's face came to mind again.

Damn it.

I tried to get him out of my head. I couldn't. I played with my breast as my husband sucked on my clit, making my body shake beyond control. *What the hell is wrong with me?* I asked myself. My husband is a great lover *what the fuck am I thinking?* Our love making was just as intense as the night before. I had the love marks on my neck to prove it. However, there I was again the next morning at the computer composing an email to him.

Dear Calvin:

I wasn't quite sure if I was going to contact you, but you definitely got my attention and are invading my thoughts. I must say I want trouble with you and I don't feel guilty about it. The only thing I'm feeling is butterflies and I want to see you when you come back to New York.

Alexis

I signed my name to the email and hit the send button before I changed my mind. After sending the email I paced back and forth wondering if he would respond and how soon the response would be? Now I became nervous *what if he doesn't respond? What if he had second thoughts? Was I making a fool of myself?* All these questions played over and over in my mind. Trying to get Calvin off my mind I reached for my cell phone to call my husband. Maybe it was my guilt but I needed him to know I loved him.

He answered on the second ring.

"Hey, I just called to tell you thank you for the amazing sex last night and also to tell you I love you more than life itself."

I could feel my husband smiling from ear to ear as he replied back "I love you too and the sex was great. I want to give you some more. I'm craving for you" he cooed into the phone.

I smiled this time and we said our goodbyes. I hung up the phone satisfied and looked back at the computer and there it was a reply from Calvin.

Holy shit...

I was scared to open it. My hands shook as I used the mouse to gear me to open it. It read:

Dear Alexis,

I have to say I was surprised to see an email from you. I honestly thought you weren't going to email me. I must admit, I am extremely happy you did. Shit I'm ecstatic and wondering how we will work out seeing each other. I live in VA but am down in New York a lot on business. Let's keep in touch with each other and make this happen. I can't wait to see you and get in your kind of trouble.

Sincerely Calvin

Shit, I almost came in my panties. I didn't know what the protocol was. I've been married for fifteen years. I haven't been in the dating scene in a very long time. I picked up the phone; I needed to hear his voice. I was creaming in my panties while the phone was ringing. *Fuck he excited me.* He answered on the third ring, "Calvin Washington,"

Damn he sounded sexy as hell. "Hello Calvin this is Alexis, how are you?"

"Wow. To what do I owe the pleasure of speaking to you? I'm impressed and shit, you sound so fucking sexy on the phone" was his response.

I was smiling and found my hand in between my legs. I ran my fingers on my sweetness just kicking the breeze with him. We were trying to figure out what we could do. I'm sure he had no clue I was actually masturbating as we were speaking. *Damn* just the way he spoke made me insane.

We talked on the phone for about an hour and I had cum about four times by the end the conversation. We made plans to see each other when he was scheduled to be in New York City in November.

True to our word we linked up at Starbucks just to kick it. I found myself salivating at the mouth as he spoke to me. I wasn't the least bit nervous and I don't know why. *Shit,* I should have been since we were in my home-town. I had a lot to lose but for whatever reason I wasn't. We talked a bit before we decided to get something to eat. It was a cold brisk day in Manhattan; he grabbed my hand as we headed to Fifth Avenue. At the corner I stopped and got in front of him.

I said to him "Can we just go ahead and get this out of the way?"

I tongue kissed him on the corner. People were staring, I didn't care. His tongue in my mouth sent my temperature rising to the highest degree. My panties became moist as my pussy throbbed in hunger for him.

He was wowed and said "Well it's a good thing we got that out of the way." We proceeded to walk to find a place where we could actually sit down and eat. We decided on Ruby Tuesday's. I must admit after we got seated, sitting across from him was driving me crazy. What I really wanted was to be sitting on top of him riding him. We spoke about our situations and how we needed to be very careful as we both loved our spouses.

Yeah I know, you're wondering by now, like how is it possible?

It is possible, we are both happily married yet we found ourselves sitting across from one another. Once we ate, he still had time because his bus didn't leave till one in the morning so we opted to do a movie. Once inside the movie theater I found I couldn't keep my hands to myself. I leaned in kissing him, grabbing at him, *shit* I wanted to fuck him then and there. After all, *what are we waiting for* were my thoughts? During these things my hands reached down and measured his dick. His dick was a nice size. How I wished

I could have slid it into my mouth at that given moment. However, there were people in the theater.

The movie ended and he said to me "God Damn Alexis you are driving me fucking crazy, I wanna make love to you in the worst way."

I smiled and responded "We always got next time seeing it's the end of the evening for you." He smiled and we both agreed we'd speak soon.

I drove him to the Port Authority and we gave each other a passionate kiss. I went home smiling and horny. My husband was asleep which I was glad because he wouldn't question me about my whereabouts. My pussy was on fire and I needed dick so I climb into the bed fantasizing Calvin was in my bed instead of my husband. I placed his soft manhood into my mouth and sucked till it rose to the occasion.

My husband began to moan "Damn Mami, I love you. I love when you suck on my cock." I kept my eyes closed envisioning Calvin's manhood. It was definitely at lot bigger than my husbands and *shit* I sure as hell couldn't wait to feel him inside of me.

I made love to my husband's dick to the point of no return. He ejaculated in my mouth and lifted me up to have my pussy directly on his face above his tongue. He ate me out as I grinded my pussy all over his mouth. I played with my breast and arched my head back as I came down his throat. After that, he moved me off of him and placed me on all fours, my favorite position.

I loved this position because I didn't have to look in his eyes knowing full well I was already cheating on him without having done anything that particular night. It soon would come and I didn't want my husband to see any guilt in my face. He made love to me till we both dropped on the bed in sweat and more cum. Our sex life is great and I had no idea what the fuck I was about to get into and I really didn't care.

Two weeks later Calvin was scheduled to come to NY on some business and his meeting was on a Saturday in Jersey City. He didn't have to be at his meeting till one, but, he decided to come very early in hopes we could *hook up*. We had spoken several times and both agreed we would meet at a hotel in Jersey.

I was nervous as hell because I knew exactly what I was going to do when I met with him. We didn't need to wait. We both had separate lives but, wanted each other. The attraction was intense between us and the sparks definitely were flying. Well, here I was in my Escalade driving to Jersey with my sunglasses on trying to hide who I am. I told my husband I was meeting with the girls to have a girl's day. He would never question me on it. I was grateful and guilty at the same time. My guilt didn't stop me from going.

I arrived in Jersey within the hour at the Marriott. Calvin was already there waiting for me in the hotel lobby. As soon as I entered I saw him, he looked good. He had on some jeans with a nice button down shirt and a blazer. *Shit.* I thought to myself. I couldn't wait to get upstairs and see what the hell he was working with.

My body was alive and awaiting his touch. "Hola Chulo," I greeted him with a kiss on his lips. He smelled fucking delicious. My heart was racing as I turned my phone on vibrate mode. I didn't want any interruptions.

We arrived upstairs. He opened the door to the room. We entered. The room was beautiful. He felt I was jittery and asked me if I was okay.

I smiled at him and said "Yes. I'm okay just a tad bit nervous." Although, I was there with him I never had cheated on my husband so my guilt was playing heavily on my mind.

He responded to me "Well, hopefully I can relax you a little." He was just as nervous, he too had never cheated on his wife. He kissed me as I leaned against the wall and *damn*, it felt so right I didn't want him to stop.

I wore jeans with a sweater and my boots, however, underneath the heavy clothing was a matching La Perla set awaiting him. He began to undress me as I stood there shaking. He did it with such tenderness making sure I was okay each time he removed an item. Once I was down to my bra and panties he was astonished because my body is fit and it doesn't even look like I bared three children. Not a stretch mark in sight. He was pleased as he twirled me around to get a good look.

"Fuck, you look great for a woman who has three children" he said.

I smiled and started to unbutton his shirt, *Oh my goodness* were my thoughts, his chest was so firm and he owned a six pack. His arms chiseled, he took very good care of himself and I must say that I was pleasantly pleased. His chest full of soft hair and his scent was driving me insane. We were kissing passionately as he led me to the bed.

He whispered "Alexis are you okay?"

I was more than okay. I begged "Calvin make love to me."

Calvin laid me down. He started at my feet, kissing them softly and up my calves with subtle pecks. The moment he was in between my thighs I moaned, my honey was dripping into my panties heavy.

He took a deep breath inhaling my essence as he removed my panties and said "Damn girl your pussy smells sweet." He teased me with his tongue slowly twirling it around my lips and clit. I was shaking beyond control the mere fact he was showing me his tongue skills had me going. I felt my juices coming down my tunnel as it reached his lips and tongue. He devoured me and swallowed as he placed my entire pussy in his mouth sucking and licking at the same time.

He played with my nipples as I screamed, "Aye Papi, que rico. Damelo de eso Papi... Hazme el amor…."

Calvin didn't speak of lick of Spanish nor did he understand it. However, it drove him crazy to hear the words coming out of my mouth.

He picked up his pace thrusting his tongue deep into my pussy and sucking on my clit making it hard. I tried to inch away from him as I felt another rush coming from within. He grabbed onto me not trying to let me get away. I screamed "Aye Dios Mios." He was bringing me to a pleasure point I had never reached. I grabbed the sheets, panting as the flood waters was rushing and creating a spray. He didn't move away at all, he wasn't afraid of it. I reached for his manhood which was standing to attention, stroking it as he drank what was left of my cum.

He moved on top of me and said "Mmmmm, Alexis you taste as sweet as you look." He placed a condom on his dick and inserted his manhood deep inside of me.

My body trembled as I connected with his rhythm. We moved in union while looking into each other's eyes. It was a surreal feeling, something I've never experienced even with my husband. Calvin was excited. Once I wrapped my legs around his back, it was a wrap. He screamed as he was cumming. He tried to pull out of me. I held my legs tighter onto his back moving my lower body in circles. He screamed and grunted as he ejaculated. He pumped a few more times and literally had to take a break.

He looked at me and apologized "Alexis you excited me, I'm sorry I came so quick. You know how to work your girl and it was driving me crazy." I smiled. I knew how to wake his manhood again. He was lying on the bed and it was now my time to show him the tigress I really was and showcase my skills. I took the condom off of him slowly.

He looked at me, smiled and asked "Alexis what are you about to do?"

I gave him a wicked grin and said "I can show you better than I can tell you." He grunted with pleasure.

We kissed each other with the same hunger from the moment we entered the room. I worked my way down to his neck, sucking softly as my hair caressed him sending goose bumps throughout his body. I sucked on his nipples while he moaned. He whispered it was his spot. I teased his nipples with my tongue, then biting them softly. Licking down his stomach I stopped above his dick which was already hardening.

I looked at him seductively then placed his manhood in my mouth. While sucking I was bobbing my head up and down slowly, keeping my eyes on his reactions. I licked the sides of his shaft, all these things proved to be doing the job; his dick was hard as a rock. I took the tip in my mouth making sure my teeth didn't scrape him. I stroked the bottom of his shaft as the tip stayed in my mouth. It was driving him crazy.

He screamed "fuck.....' He begged for me to sit on his dick.

I grabbed a condom, opened it and placed it in my mouth. *Damn I hope I can remember how to do this* I thought to myself. I slid that bad boy on his dick like a pro *just like riding a bicycle you never forget…*

He voiced how impressed he was with my skills. I gladly sat on top of his rod, taking all eight ½ inches of him. I rode slowly at first watching the intensity in his eyes, savoring the moment of making love to him. I began to contract my muscles down below working on his dick. He held onto my hips and moved with me.

I hit my spot and creamed all over him, screaming "me gusta." He began to push me harder onto his cock. *Ummm* I thought to myself *just the way I like it, rough. It couldn't get any better than this* so I thought. Calvin wanted control of the situation as he tried to lift me up. I pushed his chest back down on the bed. *No way* I wasn't gonna let him move, it was my turn to show him what I was working with.

He smiled and said "Oh I see you want to take control."

I grinned, arched my back, grabbing onto my breast to play with my nipples. He began to pant and beg for me not to stop. I pounced on his dick, rushing up and down on it.

I turned my backside to him while riding on his dick as he grabbed my ass. He held on tight as I moved up and down on him, taking every inch of him inside. I felt him in my stomach. I contracted a few more times knowing exactly what it would do to him. I felt his body begin to tremble, watched his toes curls. I smiled and turned to look his way and said "Dame eso Papi"

He lifted me off of him this time and placed me on all fours and entered me doggie style. *Fuck*, I immediately released as he pumped deep inside of me. My pussy was getting sore from his dick but it didn't matter. I loved it; I've longed for dick like this.

He screamed "Alexis" I bounced back on his dick harder, he dropped down on me and held me tight as he came once again…

He rolled off of me and looked me in my eyes, putting his thumb in his mouth. I laughed as he said "Damn Alexis that shit was fucking good."

"Uh huh," was all I could say. Then we heard my phone vibrating.

I jumped up to see who was calling me; it was my husband *fuck, just my luck*. I didn't answer I sent him to voice mail with the quickness. I became nervous and my guilt started to weigh on my mind.

Calvin looked me in the eye "Alexis don't worry we will be careful. We both have a lot to lose." He was right. We did have a lot to lose. I thought to myself *I must be out of my damn mind standing naked with Calvin. We just finished making love.*

It was time to go. I decided to jump into the shower. Calvin asked to join me. While we washed the scent of us off one another we talked. I knew from that moment I wasn't going to give Calvin up. I would keep him my *dirty little secret*. I loved my husband, and he loved his wife it was just our sexual chemistry that brought us together.

We kissed each other goodbye then he headed to his meeting and I went to find a mall. After all, I did have to go back home with some bags to prove that I was indeed out with the girls. Retail therapy was needed anyways. Just maybe it would take my mind off of me cheating on my husband. Calvin texted me and asked when could he see me again. I texted back, when you are back in NY?

Yes, we have a lot to lose but it will not stop us from seeing each other and visiting the Hotel Rooms of Jersey City or even New York....

Arrested
Monica Martinez

$\mathcal{I}$ had to be doing at least eighty on the highway, listening to house music, bopping my head. There wasn't any traffic but why would there be any at two in the morning. I was coming from a dinner dance that night. I was wearing a short beaded dress from BeBe. It showcased my cleavage. I smiled thinking about how all the women at the party gave me such dirty looks the moment I walked into the venue.

This month my hair was dyed jet black. I get bored very easily. I had on high silver pumps to match the silver beads on my dress. I stand 5'3, weighed almost 130 lbs last time I checked. I'm fair skinned; my eyes are one of my sexiest features. They are light brown, not quiet hazel, slightly slanted. When I put eyeliner on they are mesmerizing.

Jungle Brother's, I'll House You was blasting from the radio. I was singing along…

"Girl, I'll house you girl, I'll house you/girl, I'll house you/you in my hut now, my hut… When you're in my hut/you know what's up/ let your mind be free/relax your body/ jump, jump, a little higher/ jump, jump until you get tired/house your body/house your body/ house your body, to the bass/house it all over the place/don't let nobody in your way/tonight's your night, today's your day/Afrika won't steer you wrong/say what…?/house music all night long…"

I pushed the petal bringing my speed to ninety singing along with the JB's…

The car came out of nowhere, the lights and sirens blaring behind me. *Damn*, I thought. *What the hell am I going to do?* I immediately pulled over to the side. The cop car pulled behind me.

I reached to get my registration I knew I was in trouble. I had no business going that fast. I looked into the rearview mirror and saw him exiting the patrol car. He was tall. I could tell he was fit. I couldn't see his face because of his silly trooper hat. He approached my car and tapped on the window. I lowered it as he leaned down to talk to me. He waved his flashlight into the car.

Our eyes met, he was the sexiest officer I'd ever seen. His badge read Officer Sanchez. He smiled at me.

"Ma'am I need to see your licenses and registration. Do you know how fast you were going?"

I replied. "I'm sorry officer. I can't really tell you how fast I was going. I wasn't looking at the speedometer."

I felt the heat of the light on my breasts.

He was checking me out.

"Where are you coming from?" Officer Sanchez asked.

I quickly answered him, "A company function."

"Were you drinking Ms...?"

I answered, "No officer. I don't drink."

The light moved down my dress to my legs. I immediately became wet. I can't tell you what it was but I got excited. He licked his beautiful full lips and asked for me to step out of my vehicle. I did as he requested. The attraction was evident on both our behalves.

He stood at least 5'10. His body was immaculate. I licked my lips and apologized for speeding. He looked me over and complimented my dress. I thanked him. Our eyes locked onto one another again. He came closer to me.

"Why is such a beautiful young lady like you dressed this way?"

"Officer, I was at a company party. How else should I

have dressed?" I looked him in the eye and decided to go full speed with my flirting skills. *Shit*, I wanted him. It was now or never. I chuckled. "Officer Sanchez, you might not believe this but I'm actually single and have been for over a year."

The officer replied, "Hmmm… I see. Do you normally dress like this for company functions?"

"Well the parties happen occasionally."

"You look amazing."

I smiled, thanked him for the compliment then asked. "So, are you going to arrest me?" I put my hands together bringing them in front of my thighs.

He knew I was flirting.

"No. Do you want to be arrested?" He asked.

"Only by you," I answered.

He asked me to turn around so he can frisk me to see if I had any weapons. I gladly turned around, putting my hands on top of the hood of my car. I spread my legs wide. I felt him come closer to me. He turned the flashlight off. *Damn*, I felt the heat coming from his body. Mind you, it was hot outside, had to be at least eighty five degrees. He started with my upper body, patting me down and frisking me.

By the time his hand reached my breasts my nipples

were erect. He caressed them, pinching them. I gasped as my pussy throbbed and my nectar seeped into my panties.

"Mmmmm," I groaned, "Officer. Do you frisk everyone like this?"

"No Ms."

He brought his hands to the middle of my back. He took his right leg and spread my legs even further apart. *Damn* I was going to scream if he continued to tease my body. His hands moved to my 24" waist. He grunted as he moved over my round plump ass, where he lingered and whispered, "Fuck..." He then proceeded down my right leg. "Your skin is so soft," he whispered.

I moaned with delight at each touch from him.

He moved back up my right leg to my inner thigh. "Damn Mami, I can feel the heat from you."

"You have no idea" I replied.

He rubbed his finger against my soaked panties pushing against my fat pussy. He moved to my left leg and repeated the same moves. *Cono*, how I wanted him to ram his dick in me right there. Once he was done searching me he turned me around and kissed me with such force. I grabbed his hands and placed them on my tits. He began to rub on them. He moved his lips to my neck. He was hot as hell. I took his hat off of him and threw it on the pavement.

He was a fine Papi Chulo, his hair jet black which complimented his Olive complexion. His features were just as beautiful. Nice high cheek bones and a straight nose. Those fucking lips of his were so full and sexy. Even his smile was sexy. I was in heaven.

He reached for his belt and took his handcuffs off and brought them to his chest.

"Ms.," he said. "I'm afraid I'm going to have to arrest you," with a wicked look on his face.

"Oh…? Officer, please do," was my response.

He placed the cuffs on me and told me to move aside. He turned my car off and went to turn the squad car off. After that, he grabbed me to take me to the other side of my car so we wouldn't be in eyes view.

He told me to raise my hands and assume the position. I was going crazy. I wanted him to fuck the shit out of me already. Officer Sanchez got on his knees and began to frisk me again with such tenderness. He began to kiss my calves and work his way up my dress where he began to kiss my inner thighs.

My body began to tremble as he moved to my panties. He applied pressure on my sweetness with his tongue, flicking it back and forth. I screamed with pleasure. He moved to my inner thighs again kissing with soft pecks. He brought both of his hands to take my panties off of me. I stepped out of them without skipping a beat. I needed to feel the warmth of his tongue along my swollen slits.

He palmed my ass in his big hands and buried his face into my pussy with my clit in his mouth. My juices came fast, gushing into his mouth. He gladly drank without pausing. He flicked his tongue to and from my clit, down to my deep dark hole.

I moaned calling out, "Aye Papi! Just like that, yes, give it to me just like that…"

He proceeded to spread my ass cheeks further apart. He jabbed his tongue deep in my ass, licking it. Shit, he was making me hornier by the minute. I couldn't reach for him because of the handcuffs. I was reaching another orgasm because his tongue game was defiantly on point. I was moaning with delight.

He gave my ass a slight tap. I came instantly. I couldn't believe this was actually happening. Officer Sanchez moved towards the middle of my back. He stood, turned me around, and kissed me while unbuckling his belt.

He took his member out and it touched my belly. It was as hard as a rock. I couldn't wait for that mother fucker to enter me. Office Sanchez lifted me on top of his cock. He entered me and I damn near lost my mind. He held me against the car pumping deep inside of me. The beads from my dress were making music along with his strokes. I came as he hit my g-spot and screamed bloody murder. I'm loud when the dick is good and *God Damn*, his dick was good. I started to bounce on him with my hands around his neck, still in cuffs. This limited shit was getting on my nerves, I thought. I wanted to touch him, grab at him. He thrust his tongue into my mouth as he continued to pound me.

He lifted me off of his hard cock turned me around and entered me doggie style. I cried for more.

He pushed deeper inside of me telling me, "Take that fucking cock. You like it like that?"

"Aye, si, Papi si," was my response.

He smacked my ass and then grabbed it apart. He spit directly down into it and that shit fucking excited me more. How the fuck does he know me so well were my thoughts. It was almost as if he were reading my mind. He inserted a finger into my hidden quarter pleasure. I came instantly, screaming yet again. He pulled my ass cheeks further apart and sent salvia down the crack once again. I begged him for more. Taking his hard cock from my pussy he entered my ass. I came instantly as the tip went in. Soon enough his entire cock was in my ass, pumping deep into it. I groaned and screamed as he gave me some good dick.

"Fuck your ass is tight! I'm gonna cum…!" He yelled.

I begged for him not to stop. He grabbed my tits in his hands pinching my nipples. I felt his cock grow more. He began to pump faster as he released his cum inside of me. I came along with him…

Once he was done, he held on tight to me.

I turned my head to him. "Officer Sanchez, you are fucking amazing."

He smiled and kissed me on the lips.

He un-cuffed me and walked me to my car.

"Mrs. Sanchez I will not be giving you a ticket this evening."

I winked at him. "Honey, I'll see you when you get home mi amor."

I love my husband.

Day Dream

Monica Martinez

Have you ever met someone and instantly knew you wanted to be connected to this person sexually?

I went looking for an apartment one day and to my surprise on the very first appointment, I met one of the most attractive men I had ever seen. His name was Gary. He was the owner of the apartment. The moment we laid eyes on each other, I knew instantly I wanted him. The look in his eyes was just as intense as mine.

We glanced at each other's bodies with lust in our eyes. He spoke and I couldn't concentrate. All I thought about were those lips of his being on me, kissing me, tasting me.

I couldn't think of anything else. His lips were full. He was a very handsome man. He wasn't very tall, must have been only 5'7. He was thin with muscles. His features were one of a GQ model. He had a goatee which looked like he had just shaped it up. His skin was the color of caramel. I envisioned us on the apartment floor making passionate love...

I imagined us kissing and him disrobing me. He would put his mouth on my breast as I leaned back to enjoy it. He caresses my entire body as he grabs on my backside to bring me closer to him. I moan, letting him know how good it feels, how I don't want him to stop. He continues to take the rest of my belongings off while exploring my body. He stops at my belly button, kissing my stomach ever so softly while I let out a gasp. Beg and plead with him, "please don't stop..."

He proceeds to go down further to the tip of my panties, my sweetness is wet. I'm excited, wanting him badly. He turns me around to enjoy the view of me in the nude. Grunting he lifts me and takes me into the bedroom. He places me down on the big bed and spreads my legs apart, taking in my sweetness in his mouth. I am wowed by how good his tongue feels. I scream with pleasure...

I can't believe I'm there doing what I'm doing with

him. Yet I feel so comfortable, not minding I just met him. I'm here is all I can think. I make the most of it. I stop him from tasting my juices. I motioned for him to lay on the bed with me with a finger. His shirt is already off. I enjoy the fact his body has muscles galore. He is driving me crazy. He jumps on the bed with his boxers still on but his nature is fully erect. I get overly anxious and excited. As I reach for his dick, it is hard and big. All I can think is how much I'm going to enjoy him…

I teased him a bit. I bite him softly through his boxers. He moaned. I knew he wanted more, I looked him in the face.

He said. "Take it, do what you want with it."

I took him into my mouth licking the tip, amazed by the girth. He tasted deliciously sweet. He moaned with pleasure. I lingered tasting and exploring him. He grabbed my head and began to push his hardness deeper into my mouth. Exploring the back of my throat; he grinded his hips, pushing his strength deeper making me gag a little. I started to suck harder on him. I lifted a hand, brushed my hair away from my face.

I no longer wanted to wait, I pushed him down and

climbed on top of him and began riding him. As I slide his nature into my sweetness, I instantly released nectar onto him. I continued to ride him enjoying the feelings inside of me. I leaned my head back grabbing my nipples, pulling on them one by one while he stared at me and licked his lips.

He said, "I love the view from here."

I grinded, taking him completely inside of me. Damn, I felt his dick in my stomach. I had to use this to my advantage. I started to move forward and backward grinding deep hitting my g-spot. I screamed with ecstasy, releasing once again.

He grabbed my breasts and started to play with my nipples. He came to kiss me while I was still riding him. He pushed me closer into him and moved faster. I grabbed his head, pushed my tongue deeper into his mouth, showing him how much I wanted him. He lifted me up and down onto his nature with his strong hands. His nature was hard filling my sweetness like nothing has ever before. I didn't want our session to end, I thought to myself.

He took me to the edge of the bed where he laid me. He gets onto his knees taking my pearl in his mouth licking then sucking. He moved his tongue in circles, pushing deep into my pussy. I couldn't believe I've finally found someone I can truly connect with. *How can a stranger make me feel this way?* I think. I brushed the thought out of my head, I wanted to continue enjoying the pleasure he's giving to me. I moved my sweetness with the motion of this tongue. He inserted a finger while he ate me. I arched my back as he moved back to my clitoris. He started sucking and licking fast.

I screamed, "Please don't stop."

He inserted another finger bringing me to another breaking point. My legs trembled. I felt it coming again.

I warned him, "I'm going to explode…"

He continued to go faster and faster taking all my juices. My entire body arched as he grabbed me with both of his hands holding onto my pussy. He continued eating her. I screamed as my body releases into his mouth. My entire body shook uncontrollably and then while this was happening, he inserted his nature into me. I grabbed at the sheets which were off of his bed at this point. He started to stroke me hard going deep into my tunnel. I moaned begging for him to give it all to me. He continued to stroke me harder. He leaned forward to kiss me. Our bodies picked the same rhythm. I thought to myself; can it get better than this? I heard him calling my name while I was enjoying the sensations…

I felt his arm tugging at mine a little harder. He woke me from my day dream. I was embarrassed for the moment.

"Are you alright?" He asked with some concern in his voice.

I was blushing. "I'm fine. I was just off in fantasy land." I said with a smile.

He showed me the rest of the apartment.

We ended with a handshake and me telling him I would be in touch with him if I was interested in the apartment.

I left with a big smile on my face thinking to myself, sure would have been something if I actually acted on it.

Oral Delight

Monica Martinez

We went out for drinks in NYC. I was feeling good and invited him back to my place. We left the bar and headed to the subway. I live in Brooklyn, in Park Slope. It was two in the morning when we got on the F train. No one was really on it, except one lady I noticed. She was young and looked like she was just coming from a party herself. I admired her shoes.

We sat close to the empty conductor's booth. I wanted Jimmy in the worst way. We've been dating for three months. *It's about time we get it on* I thought as I leaned over and kissed him. While kissing him I placed my hand over his jeans grabbing his dick, wanting to make it hard. I anticipated this day and I wanted to feel his nature inside of me finally. Filling me and letting my 'girl' below wrap around him.

He looked at me and said "Woman you better know what you're starting" as he smiled at me.

Damn he was the definition of sexy I thought to myself.

Jimmy 5'11, 185 lbs of muscles, not an ounce of fat on him. He has a tattoo around his neck, he has a fade and no facial hair, his lips are full and his features are amazing. His face has a chisel look. He could be a model.

I continued to rub on his jeans and kiss him. His pipe got as hard as a rock. I licked my lips with anticipation wanting to taste him. I stood from my seat and bent down on my knees in front of him. It was a short ride home. I knew I could provide some oral delight, showcasing my skills. I looked back over my shoulder and noticed the young lady wasn't facing us. I pulled his shaft out of the zipper and I licked the tip softly.

I was enjoying the fact he was watching me. He started to caress my back telling me how he wanted me. I took his hardened dick deeper into my mouth. He closed his eyes. He moaned in a whisper because of our situation. "Aye Judy…" he said.

I contracted the muscle in my mouth moving his hard

dick in and out. My strokes became harder then faster. He opened his eyes, stared at me and then closed them once again.

He whispered, "Damn ma you're sending tingling sensations through my entire body."

Shit he tasted good, I didn't want to stop. His dick was growing with each lick and each suck. He begged for more. I took him as much as my mouth allowed me to without gagging. His dick had to be at least seven to eight inches. My saliva started to run down the sides of his rod; leaving his jeans wet. The train began moving at a faster pace. He was at his peak, about to give me some juice. I could tell because his legs started to shake. He started to grunt then released inside my mouth.

"I can't believe how good that felt. Your tongue game is amazing."

I moaned as I enjoyed the taste of him. I continued to suck until all his fluids were gone. I watched as his body jerked in the chair with pleasure.

I took his dick and placed it back into his jeans. He gave me a wicked grin. We were almost at our stop.

I told him "We will finish this at my place." I noticed the young lady who was on the train was looking at us in awe. She gave us a round of applause. I looked at her and smiled playfully bowing my head. We headed off the train to my place to 'finish' what I had started…

Going to Puerto Rico

Monica Martinez

They rushed off early in the morning to JFK, all packed and excited. Both were wearing sweats, it was the easiest thing to put on and plus they wanted to be comfortable. The two were sitting, waiting to board their plane. Omar and Lisa were exchanging some quick pecks with little suggestive moans in between. Lisa started whispering in Omar's ears, telling him dirty little things. Telling him she wanted to sit on his manhood teasing the tip of her pussy with it.

He would respond, "Oh yeah how so?"

Lisa would reply, "I can show you better than I can tell

you."

She was awakening his pipe with her words of lust. She noticed it was rising inside of his sweatpants. She wanted to touch it so bad but really couldn't because of all the people in the airport.

He had to get directly behind her because his dick was hard. He didn't want anyone to see him like that. Lisa was giggling as they boarded the plane and kept finding it amusing till they found their seats. Once seated the both of them kissed again.

Lisa moaned softly telling him, "I can't wait till we are in Puerto Rico making love on the beach and in the pool."

He said, "Woman, you keep it up. I may have to take care of this before we reach our destination."

Lisa winked at him "I dare you."

Omar ordered a drink because he didn't like to fly.

They were holding hands during the take off. Omar rubbed against her outer sweatpants touching Lisa where her sweetness was. Lisa started to grind her pussy closer onto his hands gasping.

He whispered "You want this?"

She looked him in his eyes "Hell yeah, I want that."

"Show me."

Lisa took his hand and put it inside of her sweats because she wanted him to feel her wetness. Once the plane was high enough and the pilot indicated that it was ok to take off the seatbelts Omar popped the little serving table down to block others from viewing what he was doing. He inched his finger within her sweats to her clit and began rubbing on her pearl.

She tried to move her body in her seat to his motion.

"Damn I want to fuck" Lisa whispered in his ear.

"Fuck it let's go to the bathroom. Let's do this." He dared her.

She quickly rose and headed toward the bathroom. He stood behind her and followed suit.

The bathroom was cramped inside but they didn't care. Both just wanted to fuck. They couldn't take the teasing anymore. Once inside he quickly pulled her pants down. His dick was already outside of his sweats. He lifted one of her legs and inserted his dick in her. They wasted no time.

He was fucking her hard and fast while she tried to hold onto the little sink with all her might. She cried out a plea of delight knowing the people could hear her outside.

She started talking dirty to him. "Fuck that pussy. Come on Papi, give it to Mami. Give it to her till she's sore."

His dick was throbbing and growing harder by the minute. She asked for more and for him to go deeper.

Lisa knew he was at his peak because of the situation. His adrenaline was pumping just as hard and fast as he was. He started to pant and grunt all at the same time. He came to pleasure, filling her dark hole with all of his hot juice. Lisa moaned as the hot splash hit her wet walls…

He dropped to his knees he was still in the mood to indulge her. He started sucking on her clit while finger fucking her. Just as she was about to explode with pleasure they heard a knock on the door.

She muttered, "Be right out…" not really caring about whoever was outside the door.

She pushed her pussy deep onto his face and held onto his head as tight as she could. She exploded her berry juice into his mouth with a sigh of relief.

Lisa whispered to him how much she loved fucking him. The banging on the door became harder, they figured they better be done now.

Lisa cleaned up what little mess they had created in the bathroom. She fixed her clothes and hair.

Omar fixed his dick and opened the door. He exited

first with Lisa trailing behind him. People were staring at them knowing full well what they were doing.

The both giggled as they sat back in their seats not giving a fuck. They waited for the plane to land in Puerto Rico…

Lisa looked at Omar in his eyes. "I tell you, it was amazing. Everyone should experience such a thing."

Well worth the trip.

Pearls

Monica Martinez

Featured in Posh Magazine February 2007

I'm home alone and it is quiet. I want to call you but decided against it. With you on my mind I go up the stairs to my room and close the door, reminiscing about you, the way you make me feel. How our sexual chemistry is on fire when we are together. My nipples are erect just from the thought of you. Standing in front of the mirror I start to disrobe. I enjoy the view of myself in my panties. I didn't wear a bra today…

…As I lay on the bed my panties are moist, just from

the thought of you. Reaching inside my night stand I take out my pearl butterfly.

Closing my eyes the pearl butterfly turns on with the click of a button. The tip of the head is moving around slowly as it reaches my sweetness. I bring it closer to go deeper...

...it's swirling.

I imagine you on top of me. I'm moving myself with the motion of the pearls in the butterfly; grinding my hips, taking the pearls completely inside of me. I start to moan. I grab my left breast, imagining you were caressing it, sucking on me softly. Thinking about your nature, how it feels inside me, inside of my mouth. I thrust the pearl butterfly harder inside of me...

...My moans become louder. I start to pant. I turn on the stimulator of the pearl butterfly where the tentacles of the butterfly touch my clitoris. This feels good, I'm sure to reach my orgasm within a few minutes. Thinking about your lips on my sweetness, reminiscing about the way you make me feel, which is marvellous. I am there at the pleasure zone. I'm reaching ecstasy. I'm imagining your nature filling me. My body shivers with pleasure as my nectar drips onto the butterfly. My sweet nectar has dripped down onto my bed...

...created a wet spot...

...I lay in the mess I made, for a moment, with a smile on my face, a wicked one. Imagining your nature is in front of me. I then take my butterfly to my mouth to taste my juices. Thinking I'm sucking my juices off your nature. Imagining I am bringing you to unbound ecstasy.

Intercourse
Monica Martinez

$\mathcal{M}$iriam Santos, a twenty three year old student pursuing her Masters in Business at Columbia University in NYC; was infatuated with her Business Law Professor Mr. John McCoy, ever since she laid eyes on him in January.

She stood 5'5, 160 lbs with an olive complexion, long red hair, brown eyes, freckles on her face, breasts 36C, 27 inch waist and her hips a 36. John is a tall handsome man, standing at 6'3, 250lbs, blue eyes, dirty blonde hair. John's body was impeccable because he took very good care of himself and kept in shape.

Miriam started out with subtle flirts by commenting on

his attire. John had never fathomed the idea of cheating on his wife of sixteen years. When Miriam would make a pass at him he wouldn't know how to respond. Miriam knew of his status because she had done her inquiry about him through other professors she had known.

One day during an exam Miriam waited until all the other students had left the classroom. She was still seated at her desk acting as if she was still taking the exam.

Mr. McCoy called out to her without even looking in the direction. "Miriam, how much longer do you think you need on the exam?"

She looked around the classroom, faked a shocked realization that everyone had left.

"Mr. McCoy I think I'm done" she told him.

He looked at her and asked her to bring him the test.

She started to walk down the auditorium toward him. Her breasts bounced with every step she took. Her pussy started to get wet just looking into his blue eyes.

John didn't turn his stare away like he normally would when he wanted to break eye contact with a lovely student. He returned the hunger in her eyes with a hunger of his own. He hadn't had sex with his wife in over eight months.

He knew it wasn't a crime to look in any event.

Miriam placed the exam on the desk; leaned over to display her cleavage. "I hope I pass with flying colors" she whispered with a great smile, showing all her pearly whites.

Miriam purposely wore a sweater. When she leaned onto his desk, John had noticed her peach lace bra; he also smelled the vanilla fragrance she was wearing.

She put her fingers through her hair "Mr. McCoy or should I call you Professor?"

John looked at Miriam's eyes "Please, call me John."

He took in her wondrous face and though he tried not to linger on it as long as he did, he couldn't help it. She had so many beautiful red freckles on her olive complexion. He wished he could have counted every single freckle on her cheeks and wondered if there were more throughout her body. Her lips were brown, fully glossed. He noticed she had a speck darker than her freckles; there was a mole on her right cheek.

"John I was wondering if you would like to go out for a drink with me?" "Miriam, it's against school policy. I can't go out with my student's, sort of a conflict of interest, not to mention I'm a married man."

Miriam leaned in more, getting closer to John's face. She brushed her lips against his ear "Well if you won't tell I won't" she whispered.

At that moment John's manhood stood at attention. He looked down her blouse, inhaling her fragrance once again. He looked back to her face. Her lips were two inches away from his mouth. He smelled the sweet mint of her breath. He was tempted to kiss her then and there. The lust showcased in Miriam's eyes made it hard for him to look away.

"Ms. Santos, I'm not sure I could do that. I happen to love my wife very much. I have a family. I have a job here which supports my family and I really wouldn't want to do anything to affect it."

Miriam realized he wasn't really putting up too much of a fight.

"Once again John, I won't tell if you don't. I'm not looking to interfere with either of your lifestyles. I just happen to be very attracted to you. I would love to get to know you better."

John nervously moved his face away to stare at the papers he had to grade. "Ms. Santos I really need to get back to work."

Miriam lifted herself from leaning on the desk.

"John, my phone number is on my test. Just in case you change your mind. I can see that you are a happy man.

Like I mentioned to you before, I'm not really interested in interfering with your lifestyle. However, I would like to get to know you better."

She winked at him and strutted out of his class. John watched her as his rod pulsated, pre-cum escaped onto his underwear. Jesus Christ, he exclaimed to himself.

He loved his wife Linda and their life together. He didn't miss what he didn't have for the last eight months until this very moment as he tried to adjust his swollen dick. He was going to go home and make love to the only woman in the world he loved, but he still had work to do. He stayed at the school grading the papers. Miriam's was the last paper he had to look at. In big bright red ink was her number with a little heart next to it displaying, **Call me**. He took Miriam's paper and placed it inside his desk drawer. He rushed to get home to his family. Just maybe it would take his mind off the steamy hot Latina in his school.

That night when John got home Linda was in the kitchen preparing his dinner. He walked in and immediately pushed her against the refrigerator. He kissed her with so much passion. Linda pulled away.

"John is everything okay?"

"Everything is," he replied. He started to kiss her neck.

Linda pulled away once again.

"John, please, the children are awake."

They had three children John Jr., ten, Melissa, six and Jesse, who was four.

"Okay. Well we should sneak upstairs then. Let's make love real quick before they notice I'm home."

Linda pushed John away.

"Not right now. I have way too much to do. I have to help John Jr. and Melissa with homework. The laundry isn't done..."

"Honey we haven't had sex in eight months. I need you right now."

Linda looked at John with indifference "God damn it John." "Is sex the only thing you think about? Our relationship is not based on sex." She slammed his dinner on the table "Here you go."

He looked at her in shock. It was perhaps the last straw. Linda was still beautiful in his eyes. She resembled Angelina Jolie. The exception was, her eyes were hazel and she was Columbian. He wondered when their love life became so non-existent. Linda had always been hot and spicy in their relationship. He couldn't for the life of him understand the sudden change in eight months. He sat and ate his food quietly trying to get Miriam out of his mind.

After dinner, John decided to help Linda with the children. He hoped if he could ease her stress with the children, he would be able to get it back in return. By nine o'clock everything was complete. He started Linda a bubble bath. Linda stepped into the bathroom and John began to take her clothing off. Her breasts at 36B were still firm, her belly still flat. No stretch marks on her body from their children. Her hips had gotten bigger since the children; she was shaped like a coca cola bottle. He was still very attracted to her. He caressed her breasts making her pink nipples hard.

Linda looked into John's blue eyes. They had been together for seventeen and married for sixteen of those years. He had been her first, the only man she slept with. That was until nine months ago when she had met Eric, a stock broker on Wall Street.

Linda took his hand, "Babe if you don't mind, I would like to take my bath alone."

John smiled at her and tried not to show how upset he was. Linda knew it wasn't fair but she had been dealing with guilt. She let another man invade her body and that man gave her feelings her husband could never give her. She had never experienced such electrifying sex as she experienced with Eric.

Linda was in the tub reminiscing about their morning together. After she had dropped Jesse off at the day care, she met Eric downtown at their usual spot. She had four hours to play with him before she would have to go get the kids from school and fix dinner. Once she arrived at the hotel she went to the prepaid room, got naked, and ran the shower.

Linda had been excited because she missed Eric and hadn't seen him for a couple of days. While she was showering, Eric opened the door to the bathroom. He came inside fully disrobed. He entered the shower and started to kiss Linda on the back of her neck. She turned around admiring his beautiful body.

Eric stood 5'11 weighed 150 lbs lean and fit. He was a dark skin Dominican man with deep brown eyes, full lips. Not an ounce of fat on his body, a boyish look to him with dimples in his cheeks and the whitest teeth she had ever seen. The water was pouring down on the both of them as he pushed her closer to the wall. Eric lifted her into his arms. He began to kiss her as the water cascaded down her backside. Eric hoisted her up as high as he could so that he could take her pulsating pussy in his mouth, Linda closed her eyes. She was enjoying what he was giving her and pleaded with him not to stop.

Eric pulled away bringing her down and started kissing her, giving her a taste of herself. Linda's body had been craving and wanting Eric, she hadn't seen him in a while. He turned her around; her butt was facing him. He bent her over and started to work his way down her back. Down to her heart shaped ass. He lingered for a while. He teased her with his tongue, giving her soft sensual pecks. He kissed her ever so softly as she let a gasp slip from her mouth. She wanted and needed him like an addict. He got on his knees and started to lick her pussy. Eric pulled her lips into his mouth, sucked and released on them. It was sending Linda into a place she only dreamed of. She moaned very loudly and begged for him to enter her.

Eric took his finger, placing it at the tip of her hidden quarter pleasure. He moved it slowly inside, finger popping her. He continued to lick and eat her pussy; making her ooze out cream. He brought Linda to full ecstasy once he entered her contracting walls.

Linda's entire body was trembling as Eric gave her all of him. Linda was wowed as she felt his rod in her stomach. Whispering for him not to stop, Eric moved his hips faster grinding deep into her; asking if she was enjoying his cock. Linda started to moan and pant taking her fingernails reaching for his sac. Eric groaned still with his finger inside of her ass. He was excited because Linda felt his rod pulsating and growing harder inside of her. He turned Linda around to face him when he was at his peak. He commanded her to get on her knees as he stroked his shaft. Linda dropped down to her knees.

The water running down on them was getting colder. He brought his hard rock closer to her mouth. Linda knew what he wanted from her. She opened her mouth as wide as she could, Eric released onto her tongue sending his cum down her throat. His cum was the sweetest she had ever tasted. Unlike her husband's John who's cum was very salty and bitter. She pulled Eric's hard cock deeper into her mouth and consumed every drop. He couldn't stop moaning, his body kept quivering…

…There was a knock on the bathroom door. It was John asking her when she was going to come out. She had been in there for over an hour.

"I'll be right out." Linda yelled.

She didn't realize reminiscing had taken so much of her time. When Linda came from the bathroom John was on their bed waiting.

"What's wrong with us these days? You don't let me touch you. I miss you Linda" he said.

Linda turned her head away trying to hide the guilt and the pain she was feeling…

"I've been going through some things and I'm just not in the mood."

John took Linda's face in his hands…

"Sweetheart, whatever it is, we will get through it. Our love is strong enough to conquer anything."

Linda got into the bed and turned off the light to go to sleep. She was going to see Eric tomorrow. As much guilt as she felt, Eric had filled a void in her life she had been missing. The love making he was providing was something John had never been able to give to her. Eric's dick was so big, thick and strong, unlike her husband whose dick was a lot smaller. Eric could make her cum just with his touch. John on the other hand, she had to fake many nights of pleasure. John was a wonderful man; she loved him dearly and loved their lifestyle. She had no idea how she was going to handle her situation.

John was upset and mad, he wanted to scream. He couldn't for the life of him understand what the hell was wrong with his wife. He thought they had a decent loving marriage. Three beautiful children and a beautiful home, they rarely fought. When Linda shut the light off and moved to her side of the bed, he wanted to reach for her but didn't. He didn't want her to reject him. He went to sleep frustrated not sure what tomorrow was going to bring them.

He awoke earlier than normal the next morning and headed to the campus to get an early start. When he walked into his classroom Miriam was seated in the auditorium awaiting his arrival. Obviously Miriam got an early start as well. John's first class wasn't till an hour at least. They were the only ones in the auditorium.

Her red hair was curly today and looked so lovely against her olive complexion. She wore a white dress. When John looked at her he was completely mesmerized. Miriam stood and greeted the professor with a wave. She started to walk towards him. John had taken notice Miriam wasn't wearing a bra as far as he could tell. Her brown nipples were erect and showing through her dress. His dick became hard. He hurried to put his briefcase in front of his member.

"Ms. Santos, what can I do for you? And so early in the morning I might add." John asked with a bit of sternness.

Miriam didn't say a word. She just continued to walk to him. Miriam swayed her hips side to side as if she was dancing. She had a look filled with desire. Her brown slanted eyes were saying things to John, saying naughty, nasty things. He wanted to resist but he was getting weaker by the moment. John cleared his throat.

"Ms. Santos, what can I do for you so early in the morning?"

"Professor McCoy" she said seductively "I came to see if I passed my test."

"Well, Ms. Santos, I haven't checked all the tests as of yet. You can come back later when we have class to find out."

Miriam was still moving closer to him. He could smell the vanilla fragrance she was wearing. His dick was awake, alive and pulsating in his pants. He looked at the beautiful freckles on her face, he wanted to reach out and touch her. Miriam sensed she had him and hurried getting even closer to him...

Her lips were inches away from his now. They were in front of each other.

She spoke softly, "Okay Professor, I will come back later, if that's what you really want."

They were so close they were almost connected. He could smell her breath and see her brown nipples trying to break out from the top of her dress Miriam moved in till her lips were touching his. She kissed him softly, John didn't pull away. She proceeded to give him tongue, taking his briefcase out of his hands and letting it fall to the floor. It made the loudest noise hitting the floor, both hardly noticed.

Miriam took John's hands and placed them on her waist. They continued to kiss and Miriam began grinding against his swollen rod.

"I want you" she whispered in his ear.

John lifted Miriam's dress enough to grab her ass. It was then he realized she didn't have panties on. He pushed his body harder into hers. His fingers started to explore her, roaming around to find her secret box.

Miriam gasped as John's hand found her treasure. John lifted Miriam and put her on his desk face down. He took his hard cock out of his pants and pushed deep inside of

Miriam. Miriam let out a slight cry of pleasure. He pumped deep and hard into her…

John grabbed Miriam's ass tighter with his hand as he continued to pump. It was going to be hard not to cum so fast. She was wet, warm and it felt good to John as he gripped and pulled a knuckle full of her long beautiful red curls. Miriam whimpered "Give… me… more."

John got excited and obliged but he knew he was about to erupt. "I'm going to cum." He told her between a groan and panting.

Miriam bounced her ass harder onto his dick. She grabbed her ass, spreading it apart for him; telling him to fuck her. John couldn't hold it anymore he tried to pull out. She wouldn't let him. She bounced harder onto his cock and he grunted as he filled her canal with his semen…

He stopped, realizing what he had just done and pulled out of her quickly. "Ms. Santos, I'm sorry…"

Miriam turned around to face him. Her face was the fullest naughtiest smile.

"Mr. McCoy there is no need to be sorry. I enjoyed it very much."

Miriam reached for the straps of her dress, let them loose, letting her dress fall to the floor. John looked at her. He couldn't believe what was happening.

He stepped closer to her. Miriam's vanilla fragrance was filling his nostrils. He cupped her beautiful brown breasts one by one inserting them into his mouth. He licked around them, bit them softly and swirled his tongue in circles. Miriam arched her back onto the desk and asked for more. John worked his way down her stomach then back to her neck. He whispered in her ear how beautiful she was.

The announcements started on the loud speaker, the both of them stopped and looked at each other. John took his now soft dick and adjusted his pants. He bent over to the floor, picking up Miriam's dress. He gave it back to her.

"Professor, you were fabulous." She said. Then she left and headed out to her class.

John sat at his desk looking at the picture of his beautiful wife. He put his head down. He asked God to forgive him because he didn't want to bring any pain to his family.

John couldn't concentrate. He had betrayed his wife. He needed to go back home and confess to his wife of his infidelity. He should have been more patient with his wife, awaiting her desire. Instead he did the most horrible thing in the world. What if this ruined his marriage? What would he do? How would Linda feel when he told her he cheated on her? John had to get home quickly. He needed to talk to his wife. They had to work this out. He would deal with Miriam on a different day. He would tell her he couldn't see her again. Shit maybe even asked her to change his class. The guilt started to lay heavy on his mind. It will never happen again. He thought and tried to convince himself. John stared at the wall.

John taught one class and left work afterwards. He was upset with himself, cancelled all his other classes. He got into his car. He hit the steering wheel with anger numerous times before he turned the ignition key. *Why hasn't she make love to me these last eight months?* he thought. John called Linda at the house. She didn't answer. He tried her cell phone. It went straight to voicemail.

He drove home and noticed two cars in his driveway. He thought it to be strange. He didn't like the feeling he was getting in the pit of his stomach. *Maybe it's just my nerves* he thought. He left his car parked down the block and walked. He wasn't sure why he'd done so but he had so many things going on inside him. He figured after a little walking he wouldn't be so nervous to tell her. He tried to ration with himself; all they had to do was fix their marriage and get it back to the way it was. He never would have done it, why the fuck was he so weak now? *Pussy, the root of all evil* he thought to himself.

He wondered if she would forgive him and more importantly, if he should tell her? He made his way to the front door, his heart beating fast as he opened the door...

Linda wasn't in the living room or the kitchen. He headed up the stairs to their bedroom. He heard noises coming from behind the door. John knew it was his wife screaming with such satisfaction. She was moaning the name Eric over and over again. John couldn't believe what he was hearing outside his bedroom door. He opened the door; saw a man on top of his wife pumping in and out of her. Eric and Linda were so busy they hadn't even noticed John was in the doorway. John's dick immediately got hard. He wanted to join them. His thoughts went instantly back to Miriam.

He closed the door to his bedroom. He decided to head back to the school. John walked to his car with thoughts of his wife moaning and the guy who was fucking her. His dick was pulsating. He should have made a noise and just maybe he could have joined them. He was excited. He would have put his dick into his wife's mouth while the other man continued to fuck her.

He drove faster to the school. He wanted Miriam again. He needed to find her and fuck her all over again. After all, it is just intercourse.

Phone Sex
Monica Martinez

I was horny and decided to call my girl, Maritza. She's a shorty I been banging for some time. Maritza lives in the Bronx, off of the Grand Concourse. She's 5'5 130 lbs thick. Her measurements are deliciously crazy at 34C, 23, 38; she has light brown eyes with an olive complexion and long black straight hair. She looks real exotic, like a Taino Indian. She has some luscious lips and a beautiful smile. By now I knew she was either home already or just about there. I reached for my phone to call her. I was lying down in my bed with my dick in my hand. My dick was nice and hard. She answered on the first ring.

"What up Chulo?" Her sexy voice said to me.

I said "I was thinking about fucking you."

She giggled into the phone "I was thinking about fucking you too, thinking about the last time we were together." She breathed so heavy I heard it from my phone like she'd spoken a word. "I just walked in. Let me walk up stairs."

I chuckled, cuz I was sure glad she knew exactly what I wanted, she always did. Maritza told me my voice made her horny all the time cuz it was deep. She told me she was reaching inside her dresser for one of her toys.

"Good girl." I told her. I instructed her to hop on the bed and put her toy on the pillow and to await further instructions. Then I said. "What are you wearing?"

She said, "Today I have on a pair of beige slacks, a brown sweater, and knee high brown boots."

I told her to take every article of clothing she had on, off, one by one except for the bra, panties and the knee high boots. She did as I instructed.

I asked her "What color are your undergarments?"

"I got on a cream Victoria Secrets bra, the one you love with the matching panties."

Diablo Nena I whispered in the phone "Mamita those are the panties that hug your ass so lovely." I requested her to lie back onto the bed and open her legs wide. I told her how I wanted to play and I hoped that she had her toy ready.

"Yes Papi," she responded, "It's ready." She turned on the toy to let me hear the vibrations.

I moaned and said "Baby take off your panties." Maritza got off the bed and explained to me exactly what she was doing.

She told me she was in front of the long mirror she had in her bedroom, "Papi my juices are flowing down my legs…" She teased me, giving me the details. She whispered into the phone seductively, "they are coming down my thighs and my hand just brushed against my butterfly."

Maritza moaned with pleasure.

I groaned, "Mmmmm, Mami," into the phone. I told her she was driving me crazy making those sounds.

She said, "My butterfly is throbbing and seeping. I wish you were here with me to drink from it. Papi, I'm on my bed again, laying on my back with my eyes closed. I'm playing with clit making it nice and hard." She let me know she had inserted a finger inside of her sweetness, exploring her wet walls. "Papi I'm pushing my fingers in and out of my pussy. I am reaching for my pocket rocket. I opened my legs wider. My pussy is throbbing. My nipples are erect under my bra."

The more she talked the more my dick pulsated. I began to stroke.

She informed me she was releasing her breasts from the bra and said "I'm touching my brown nipples, pulling and squeezing them, one by one."

Man, oh man I grunted into the phone and said "Mami, I'm stroking my dick. If I was there now, what would you want me to do to you?"

She responded; "If you were in front of me, I would want you at the edge of my bed licking and sucking my clitoris." Maritza told me she had her pocket rocket positioned on her clit. "I'm moving it side to side letting the metal balls hit on it sending the vibrations deep into me. Papi, my clit is so hard." She began to wail into the phone.

I whispered. "Imagine that's my tongue on your clit and my fingers are inside you while I'm eating you out."

She was panting into the phone and begging me to continue with my words.

"Baby, imagine my tongue going deeper into your canal licking and sucking all the juices around her." I told her how I would thrust my tongue all around her clit, back into her pussy.

Maritza's screamed. "My body is starting to shake. You know I love when you do that to me."

I whispered with my deep voice, "Imagine I'm holding your lips apart while I lick that pussy softly and slowly."

"I want more…" she whimpered into the phone.

I continued telling her, "I have now turned you around to eat your ass out, while I'm still playing with your clit."

Damn I know how crazy it drives her when I do this to her.

She told me she was putting the speed on the pocket rocket to full blast. Then she started screaming loudly.

"My toy is hitting me hard… I'm grinding harder and am pushing a finger deep inside my pussy. I'm almost there…" She said gasping and groaning.

"Yeah baby, bring it me. Bring it to Papi. Imagine the tip of my dick touching your pussy, teasing it."

Maritza cried into the phone. "Papi, give it to me."

"I just entered you with my dick."

"I'm arching my back, grabbing my breasts as this toy brings me to heaven. Daddy, I wish it was you, I'm cumming…" she screamed into the phone.

"Yeah Mami cum for me..." I begged.

"I drenched my bed. I came for you" she told me with heavy panting in between. "Now it's your turn to give me what I wanna hear." She whispered in a seductive voice to me. "I'm there teasing you, taking the tip of your hard dick into my mouth, licking around it, sucking hard and then releasing."

I moaned as I envisioned her actually doing it. Shorty was definitely skilled in that department.

She whispered with authority. "Spit on your dick right now."

Damn I loved when she talked like that.

My dirty girl...

Maritza told me to stroke my dick as if she were actually stroking it. She described how she would take my balls into her mouth, one by one, licking and sucking while continuing to stroke my rod. At that point I started to go crazy over the phone.

"Yeah Mami," I yelled in between pants.

"I'm licking that dick again. I'm on top right at the tip and sucking all the pre-cum" she whispered.

Fuck I begged for her to put it inside of her mouth.

"I take it in my mouth until I'm gagging…" Maritza blurted.

She could hear my heavy breathing in the phone. I was at my breaking point. She described how she was moving her head faster up and down, letting my dick explore the back of her throat. I grunted into the phone as she told me, "When you buss don't let one drop of it miss my mouth because I deep throated it. I sucked all the liquid out."

"Damn Muneca," was all I could say into the phone.

Maritza giggled.

I said "Mami I think I need a shower."

"Me too" She replied.

I hung up the phone with a smile on my face knowing that I was going to see Shorty later in the week.

For sure it's going to be some awesome sex.

Office Pleasures
Monica Martinez

I was single from the moment I got pregnant and had just given birth to my son. My baby daddy wanted nothing to do with me or my pregnancy, sad but true. I worked at St. Vincent's Hospital in Manhattan for the Chief Executive Officer. I was out on maternity leave for all of five weeks. I needed to get back to work because my financial situation was getting tight. I had worked at the hospital for three years and upon my return I bumped into Tyrone. He was the supervisor of billing and collections. He had always flirted with me from the moment he got hired about a year and a half ago.

Tyrone was about 5'9, very skinny, brown skin with beautiful full lips, and kept his hair in a Caesar look. He had a goatee, and reeked sexy with his eyebrow piercing and an earring in his left ear. His features were defined. He had a straight nose and high cheek bones. He was fine but I had this thing about mixing business with pleasure. Often enough it just never panned out. Now, working at a hospital, the ratio of women to men is about eight to two. So if you were having lunch with a male co-worker it usually meant you were fucking him. I ignored the rumors about Tyrone and me. We clicked and always did lunch together. Hell, there was even a rumor about how the baby I was carrying was his. That was definitely not the case.

We got along and yes he wanted to fuck me and the feeling was mutual; however, I never gave him any play. We would just flirt a lot. Throughout my pregnancy he would say "Tatiana you are so beautiful and I wish you were carrying my baby." He helped me go shopping and even came by my house to help set up the nursery. He was there for me when I cried about my son's father and when I told him how alone I felt. Returning to work was good for me because I was always home with no real adult talk. I just had this little newborn baby boy who just ate and slept.

Before getting pregnant my body was nice. I was a size double zero weighing all of 84 lbs at 5' and everything on me was small. My breasts were an A cup and my waist 23 inches. My butt was the biggest thing on me, it measured a 32. It was what most men called a bubble butt. I have long dirty blonde hair past my ass which is wavy, unless I blow dry it straight. My eyes are shaped like almonds and they are hazel. My skin tone is not quite olive but not white, I guess somewhere in between.

Well after giving birth to my lil man, I weighed 120 lbs and my breasts became a full firm C cup and my waist measured at 25. Eventually my belly went back to its flatness *thank goodness.* My ass has grown to a whopping 40 inches. My mother said I grew into my womanhood after giving birth to my son.

Well, bumping into Tyrone that morning, he was stunned and looked at me in amazement.

"Damn Tatiana," he said, "you look so lovely. Look at you, just giving birth and getting your body back in shape." He stared at my breasts. "Your breasts got bigger."

I laughed at him. "Silly," Then I said jokingly, "You better watch out. If anyone hears you they could say you were sexually harassing me."

We both laughed.

He grabbed my hand and twirled me around. He wanted to get a better look at everything.

"Damn baby girl, your ass got bigger too. You look really good."

When his hand touched me it sent a rush over my entire body. I blushed and looked away. Tyrone put his hand on my chin and pulled my face to look him in the eyes.

"I've missed you."

I responded without hesitation. "Oh how sweet, I've missed you too."

"No, I really missed you." He reiterated with lust in his eyes.

I became wet instantly, I pulled away from him said, gotta go.

He yelled over his shoulder "I'll see you for lunch."

I shook my head, yes.

Oh my goodness was all I could think. My heart was beating fast and my pussy thumping. I thought maybe because I hadn't had sex since getting pregnant, I was in heat. It had to be because I always had control when it came to Tyrone.

Throughout the morning I tried to do my work, but all I could think about was what Tyrone said earlier about missing me. I hadn't felt wanted in such a long time, just those words coming out of his mouth sounded so endearing.

It was my first day back and my boss was surprised to see me when I walked in. He couldn't believe I was back so soon. We caught up on all the reports he was going to need since I'd been gone for a good deal of time. I was his favorite and most efficient worker.

I left the bosses office and walked back to mine. I saw the red light on the phone on my desk, which meant I had voicemail. Tyrone left me a message telling me he was glad I was back and he couldn't wait to do lunch with me. He said he was a bit upset at me because after giving birth he tried calling me several times. I ignored his calls because I was going through my own personal issues about having a baby with no father. I was stressed.

Tyrone left me messages about being with me and us raising my son together. I ignored and deleted them. I liked Tyrone but wasn't sure about him because we joked around a lot and he was five years younger than I. I didn't think he really knew what he wanted. I thought when he said those things it was just his way of trying to get some ass. I had been there and done that in my past, listening to everything a man would say. *Shit* look at me now thinking my baby daddy was in love with me. Then he left my ass the minute I told him I was pregnant. I wasn't falling for game, no way, no how. I deleted Tyrone's message and proceeded to call him at his extension.

"Hey, Mister Man, it's 11:45a.m. I was thinking maybe we could head to the mall for lunch. I'm starving."

Tyrone replied "No problem. I'll meet you in the front, at our spot." He paused slightly then said, "You got my message?"

"Yes Ty, I got your message" I responded.

He said "Well did you listen to it?"

"Duh, of course I listened to it. I'm sorry I didn't call you while I was home. We will speak during lunch."

Tyrone and I met at twelve on the dot and headed to the mall.

He said "You know there's a rumor about your baby being mine."

"Yeah, I guess people have nothing better to do than spread lies."

"You know I don't deny it. I've told you before I wish he was mine, so you would be mine."

"Come on Ty, you already know I don't mix business with pleasure."

"What you mean? You're not attracted to me?" he asked.

"Ty it doesn't matter if I am or not, bottom line is that it's not going to happen."

Tyrone left it alone.

For the next month Tyrone and I went to lunch religiously. Each time I was with him I couldn't help but wonder what he was packing and how much I wanted to stick my tongue down his throat.

My attraction to him was evident whenever he was near me. I would divert my attention, trying not to look into his eyes. Every time I saw him I had this warm sensation going throughout my entire body. My heart would beat faster and my honey would seep out down below.

One day, I had a report which was due first thing the next morning. My boss had made it clear I needed to get it done, come hell or high water. I worked through lunch and ended up calling my mother so she could get my son from the babysitter. Only God knew when I was going to leave work. It was already five o'clock; and mostly everyone had left the office for the day. I had called Tyrone earlier in the day to let him know there was no way I could do lunch with him. I figured I would catch up with him later. As time lapsed I thought for sure he had already left the building like everybody else. I figured I'd give him a call later in the evening or just see him in the morning.

My phone rang exactly at 6:05 p.m. I had no clue who in the hell it could have been since the office was officially closed for operating hours. I answered the phone.

"Good afternoon Tatiana speaking. How may I help you?"

Tyrone said "Well you can let me swing by and see you for a minute before I leave."

I laughed "Come on by I'm still working on a project."

"No problem, I'll keep you company" he replied.

Tyrone was in my office ten minutes later. He pulled a chair next to mine and asked how my day was.

"Busy as usual."

I asked him about his day.

"Well let me see, I was busy, but, I was thinking about this shorty that won't give me play. I've been after her for over a year now. I'm single. She doesn't want me. I wonder why?"

I laughed, turned toward him on my swivel chair to

look him in the eyes.

Tyrone had this intense look. He leaned into me, kissing me softly on my lips. I didn't move, couldn't move. I just let him give me soft pecks on my lips. He proceeded to give me tongue. *Damn* it felt good. I hadn't been kissed or touched in what seemed like forever. I had on a skirt with boots and a button down blouse. Tyrone put his hands on my legs. He began to rub his hand up and down my skirt. I pulled away…

"What are we doing?" I asked.

"I'm kissing you. I want you," he whispered. "You've been putting me off for over a year. I've been trying to get at you. I ain't messing with no one here. I don't plan on ever messing with anyone except you. I know you are a good woman. I want you for me." He looked very serious as he said those things.

He leaned in to kiss me again.

I let out a small gasp. "Damn Ty…" was all I could say. I wanted him just as bad, and hell, he could definitely have me…

Who was I waiting for? What was I waiting for I asked myself? A father who didn't want to be a father to our two month old son? Tyrone stood. I didn't push him away when he pulled my chair closer to his. He moved his body in close to mine; put his hands around my waist. He started to kiss my neck, went down to the cleavage showing out of my shirt...

He left his chair and went down on his knees. He looked up at me as if he were waiting for a response.

I gave him the, I want it look.

He lifted my skirt, situated himself in a better position on the floor in front of my chair. He manipulated my legs open, and moved me back into my chair, ripping a hole in my stockings. He tore my panties off and started to thrust his tongue around my pussy. I thought for sure I was gonna cum instantly because his tongue was pierced.

Jeez this man was gonna send me into heaven with the movement of his tongue.

I moaned his name, softly. Tyrone sucked on my pearl for a few minutes, making my clit hard then thrusting and thrashing his tongue deep into my canal. My juices came flowing out like a waterfall. I held onto the chair for dear life. I hadn't been touched in almost a year, talk about being backed up. Tyrone continued to bring me pleasure for the next twenty minutes. I didn't scream because I wasn't one hundred percent sure if anyone else was in the other office. I moved my pussy around his tongue. I pushed him deep into my pussy arching my back bracing myself for another orgasm.

The orgasm was fast approaching and Tyrone knew it. He put his finger inside my pussy inching to my g-spot and hitting it fast. My body started to tremble and my juices came gushing out.

He let out a sound of triumph. "Damn, you should have let me take care of you a long time ago."

I reached for him to come from off the floor. Tyrone rose. I directed him to a part of the office where the filing cabinets were. I saw his dick was hard in his fitted jeans. *Damn he was packing.* I really didn't think he was going to have such a big dick because he was a skinny dude. I unzipped his pants. I was in complete awe. Tyrone had to be packing at least a nine inch rod and it was thick too. I was in ecstasy seeing it and it too was pierced. *Hot damn*, he was just sexified as far as I was concerned. I took his dick into my mouth sucking just the tip, playfully on his piercing. He called out my name "Tatiana" over and over again as I sucked the tip. I tried to take him deep into my mouth. I couldn't. It was hitting my throat and it wasn't even all in my mouth. I contracted my mouth on his shaft, stroking him at the same time. He held onto the filing cabinets leaning his head back and begged me to work his dick. I sucked devouring him, taking in his essence which smelled sweet. I bobbed my head up and down his shaft. Within minutes Tyrone had shot his load in my mouth. I swallowed every drop of it. It tasted delicious.

We heard someone coming towards the office. He hurried and put his hard dick away. I went back to my deck and adjusted myself back in my chair. It was Tanya from the nursing department asking for a change in payroll. She looked at both of us and asked us if she was interrupting anything. I gave her a dirty look and said no, not at all. She left after I took her information.

Tyrone looked at me, "Tatiana that's it. Its official, you are now my wifey." I laughed at him and asked. "Why? Cuz I gave you good head?"

"No because we are going to become one."

He kissed me again.

I said, "Ty, I really need to finish this work."

He asked if I wanted him to leave. I shook my head, yes.

He said "Well, call me later. I'll come by the house."

I agreed to call him once I got home. I didn't call him because I couldn't believe what had happened between us. I was embarrassed. I didn't know what he would think of me, and to be honest I was scared. I tried to avoid Tyrone for the next couple of days, telling him I couldn't do lunch.

By the third day Tyrone had shown up at my office refusing to hear no for lunch. He said "If you don't go to lunch with me I'm gonna tell everyone we are a couple and that the baby is mine."

I looked at him like he was crazy, but he looked serious. I figured I better go to lunch with him.

The first thing to come out of his mouth at lunch was, "Are we gonna talk about what happened between us?"

I said "Ty it won't work. I'm older than you. I have a newborn. Trust me; you don't want anything to do with me."

He took my face into his hands, "Tatiana, you don't get it, do you? I'm in love with you. I want to be with you. I want to be your man. I want to raise your son as ours."

Tears flowed down my face after he said those words because he said it with such sincerity.

Tyrone and I became a couple. We are still together

raising our children. That's right, you heard me correctly; we have a total of three kids. Two boys, one girl, and we got married. We still work together at the hospital. And for the record we still give oral pleasure every chance we get.

Oops
Monica Martinez

I had this chick I've been seeing on and off for a few years. She would call me to have lunch or rather to have one of our rendezvous. I was horny this one time I called her and asked if she wanted lunch. Let's just put it out there for what it really was, I wanted to fuck.

After lunch, I took her to my house. The sex was awesome every time we got together. When we got inside my house, I was going nuts. She was looking good with her tight ass jeans. Showcasing her curves, her stomach was nice and flat. She didn't have tits but it was okay with me cuz where she lacked in that area, she made up for in booty.

She was a nice hot Puerto Rican from Queens, short with nice long black hair, her eyes were slightly slanted. Her lips were full; she had a pretty smile and nice straight teeth. Shorty took care of herself, always had her nails and toes done.

Man, I wanted to drag her by her hair straight to my bedroom. However, the gentleman in me wouldn't do that to her. It wasn't always about sex with her. She was cool. We could just hang out. Truth be told, I had pussy everywhere. I never really had to push if you get what I mean.

We started kissing on the couch while watching television. I started to caress her breasts. I managed to get her bra off with one snap of my fingers. I started to suck on her nipples making them nice and erect. I moved my way back to her neck, where I lingered and sucked. My dick was standing to attention at this point. I wanted her to suck it. She never really sucked it before. She always did a few licks here and there. So I felt it was time her lips met my man, finally...

I was sitting on the couch. She was on her knees facing me. I pushed her head to my hard dick. It was already out my pants. She tried to pull away. I moved her head back towards it.

It was almost as if she was afraid of it which boggled

my mind because the sex was good. She was married before. Surely she knew how to give head you would think. I pushed my dick to her lips. She didn't budge. Actually, she turned her head away from it. I was like, what the fuck is wrong with her. I tried not to sound annoyed, "What's wrong?" I asked.

She looked at me. "Umm, I don't know how to do this."

What the fuck I thought to myself, *is she fucking kidding me?*

"What? Weren't you married before?"

She responded, "Yeah, but I didn't suck my husband's dick."

I just looked at her like she was out of her damn mind. I thought to myself *maybe it was the reason she was divorced.* I told her it wasn't really hard to do you just put it in your mouth and try not to let your teeth scrape against the shaft. She looked at me like I was crazy. I gave her the same sort of look back. I was determined to get my dick sucked, especially since I always provided her with good oral sex. I pushed my dick to her lips again. She didn't move.

She barely opened her mouth. She looked at me as she grabbed my shaft. "What am I suppose to do again?"

I explained it to her once again. I was ready for the action and getting a little aggravated. She started to lick the tip with bullshit licks. I didn't want to hurt her feelings, so when she looked at me I just shook my head, yes. Meanwhile I was thinking, *okay, where are the cameras cuz this has got to be a fucking joke.* This woman was twenty eight and I couldn't fathom the idea she's never sucked dick. *Like what the fuck. I mean yes I know Spanish women don't usually like to suck dick; but damn once in a while ain't gonna kill nobody.*

I told her to put the head in her mouth and suck like a lollipop. *I can't believe her* I was thinking, now, *how fucking juvenile is this?* She kept looking at me like a deer caught in head lights.

She said, "Please don't cum in my mouth."

I shook my head, no to make her hurry. To be honest I didn't even think I would be able to cum.

She started to get at it a little, with a scrape on the shaft here and there. She had been down on me for what seemed like an hour and her strokes became harder. The sucking became a little better or at least I had to convince myself it did. She looked at me again and reminded me not to cum in her mouth. I had to concentrate on cumming to begin with because I never had a chick who didn't know how to suck dick before. I began to thrust my dick in her mouth which probably wasn't a good idea. She started to gag. She pulled her head away from my throbbing cock. I apologized.

She said, "Eddie," With a whine. "I'm serious don't cum

in my mouth." No, I shook as I held the back of her head and stroked hard into her mouth. I couldn't help myself I knew I was cumming but she didn't have a clue.

I shot straight into her mouth. She jumped up quickly yelling at me as she ran to the bathroom to spit it out.

I yelled "Oops…. I'm sorry…" Meanwhile I was like yeah that's what you get.

She was a cock teaser not sucking on my dick before. I thought she would never speak to me again because she was so upset. She was in my bathroom spitting for at least twenty minutes, yelling, "I need a toothbrush."

I myself stayed in my living room laughing to myself. She finally came out of the bathroom. She yelled at me some more accusing me of doing it on purpose. There was no way I was going to admit to it. I apologized again. She wanted to go home.

We headed back down to the Bronx where her car was and off she went. I thought about the events of our day and was cracking up in my car.

After ten years, she now swallows like a pro and does other things she never thought she would do in a lifetime. Yeah, baby girl turned out to be my wifey and now the biggest Freak.... Now that's what I'm talking about.

Masturbation
Monica Martinez

Malik is tall, dark, handsome and sexy as hell with dreads hanging down to the middle of his back. He stands about 6'2" with abs of steel, and 225lbs of muscle rippling throughout his body. His skin is smooth and his complexion milk chocolate. His eyes are a deep dark brown, he has thick eyebrows, a broad nose; his lips, full and kissable. The clef in his chin makes him even hotter. His features are just dominating and powerful. He is everything that represents a strong black man in my eyes. I laid in my bed in complete darkness thinking about him. The thought of his long thick rod inside me was arousing. Just envisioning being with him sent chills down my spine. Malik makes love to me like no other has. I was restless one summer night. It was hot, and I couldn't get comfortable.

That evening I had only worn a tee-shirt. I moved around trying to find a relaxing sleeping position. The sheet slid in between my legs rubbing onto my clit and I let out a soft moan because it felt good. I began to rub against my linen, thinking about the way Malik touches, caresses, and kisses me. My tunnel was completely drenched in nectar as I envisioned him.

I closed my eyes and went into fantasy land imagining what we would do if we were together. My grinding became harder making the sheet saturated with my juices. I started to whisper his name as if he was there with me, "Malik, Malik…." begging for him not to stop. I grabbed my breast with one hand, playing with my nipple and imagining Malik was sucking on it, biting me softly like he does. I grinded my hips deeper into the sheets; which was definitely providing an incredible feeling. My thick flower began to throb from the good feelings I was giving to myself with thoughts of him. I imagined him standing above me with his long and thick member. Then he inserted it in my mouth. I moaned licking the tip of his hardness.

I continued to masturbate with the sheet, needing to bring myself to complete pleasure. I could feel that I was at my point and almost about to explode. Recalling a time Malik was eating me out and inserting his long hard pipe inside of me made my body tremble. I pushed the sheet deeper against my 'girl' making myself scream his name loudly. I came to complete ecstasy closing my eyes wishing he was here with me, watching as I released all of the day's tension in his name…

Booty Call

Monica Martinez

What's up, my name is Marisol and I live in Queens. I stand all of five feet, and weigh 110 lbs. The only curves I have are my hips and ass. My breasts are an average B cup. My hair is jet black, and very long, well past my behind. Many say with the dark hair against my creamy white skin I look exotic. I've often been mistaken for a white girl until I open my mouth or they see the Latina curves. Bottom line, I look good. You might think I'm conceited but it's not even the case, I'm just confident. Enough with all of that, I wanna tell you about an encounter I had. I guess it would be safe to assume we've all had this in our life at one time or another. His name was Manny from the Bronx, and he was fine as he can be. What we Boricuas would call a Papi Chulo.

I met him one day, on my lunch break when I worked in NYC. I was at lunch with some of my girls when he approached me and asked if he could talk to me briefly. I stepped to the side and let him have words with me. To be honest, from the moment I saw dude I wanted to fuck him. He stood about 5'10 about 170 lbs and muscular. He had dark black hair which was pushed back, eyes were very seductive and brown, his complexion olive. He reeked sexy. His smile could make you melt, nice white teeth to go along with it. We exchanged numbers and he called me about a week later. We hooked up, hung out a couple of times before it became sexual. Dude was a big time drug dealer; which one scared the hell out of me, and two, I knew I didn't want him as a boyfriend.

One night I was feeling so horny, I knew a toy wouldn't suffice. My pussy was on fire and needed a good pounding.

I got on the phone and beeped dude at midnight. He called back with the quickness. I spoke seductively on the phone and asked him if he wanted to come over.

He said, "Marisol, I would love to come over."

I told him I was going to take a shower and wait for him. I jumped in the shower getting excited cause I was hoping and praying like most of us do when it's the first time…

We pray the sex ain't weak and we pray dude's dick is big enough to satisfy us.

I decided to put on a hot black piece of lingerie from Victoria Secrets and threw on some red high heels. All the while my pussy was craving, wanting, waiting and throbbing. It was about one in the morning when my outside bell rang. I buzzed him upstairs. He knocked on the door. The minute I opened the door dudes mouth dropped.

He said "Wow, you look fucking sexy."

I smiled and invited him inside. He closed the door behind him; he put me against the wall. We started to kiss while he took off his coat. He lifted me off my feet and started to eat my pussy, against the fucking wall. I started to moan as my 'girl' was getting wet and enjoying his tongue.

He moved me to my dining room table while still devouring my nectar. Trust me, it was definitely feeling good. I couldn't contain myself; I began to talk dirty to him asking if he was enjoying my taste. He moaned as this excited him all the more. He inserted a finger inside of me and started to suck on my clit. I started to move my hips along with his fingers, it was driving him crazy. He took off his pants and inserted his big hard cock inside of me. I thank god for answering my prayers. Ladies, I was thrilled his dick was big. I came instantly once he put it inside of me while he was fucking me on the dining table. I screamed with pleasure. My body shivered uncontrollably and he continued to make me moan while literally fucking the shit out of me. Manny from the Bronx was blowing my back out.

It was exactly what I had wanted and needed. His stamina was amazing, he came and his dick was still hard wanting more of me. He took me off of the table, bent me over the chair and gave it to me doggy style. He pulled my hair and asked me if I liked it. I begged him for more; I didn't want to stop fucking him. Manny kept pounding my pussy and giving me his cock. I made sure to move my body along with his movements. I wanted to keep up because this was the type of sex I yearned for. He took me from the table to my bedroom, where he began eating my pussy out again and making me cum beyond belief. The pleasure he was providing was like someone who just got out of jail and had been deprived of pussy for months.

He laid me down on the bed on my belly, and again went to work on my pussy. He didn't stop until 'she' dripped and he swallowed all her juices without missing a drop. He came around to me with his big fat cock facing me and pushed the tip to my mouth. I gladly took it without any hesitation, hell I wanted to show him what I was working with and bring him to as much pleasure as he brought to me. As far as I was concerned, one good head deserved another. I sucked on him fast, like he was a meal and I was feasting. Trying to take him completely in my mouth, I couldn't, I gagged but shit I didn't care. The look on his face said it all, as to how much he was enjoying what I was doing. He grabbed the back of my head and he pushed it deeper into my throat. He grunted and his body started to tremor as he released into my mouth. It tasted good and the mere fact I excited him this way only aroused me more.

He went on my bed, on his back. I straddled him and started to ride him as his hands cupped my breast. He played with my nipples. I rode his dick like it was the last dick on earth. I moved my hips grinding all the way down. I wanted to get his rod all the way inside of me. He moaned with pleasure.

"Yeah Mami give it to me," was what he said, "give me that sweet tight pussy, give it to me."

This heightened my high even more; I spun around and gave him my back as I continued riding his manhood. He grabbed my ass and spread it apart. That shit had never been done to me but it drove me crazy.

I yelled to him "Yeah Papi do that shit to me. Fuck me…" I screamed.

He got even more excited. He lifted me a little, started fucking me harder over and over again. I creamed on his dick crazy and he loved it. He started to grunt with excitement once again. I knew he was cumming. He took me off of him and told me to take it again in my mouth. I jumped at the opportunity to bring him to full ecstasy.

Manny sat on the edge of the bed and placed me on top of him so our bodies were facing each other. We kissed with lust inside of us. Then he fucked me again. My pussy was sore but I was enjoying his skills and the way he was fucking me. He came hard yet again. We decided a shower was what we needed. We hadn't realized how much time had passed. When we headed for the shower it was already 6:00 a.m. We had been fucking for five straight wonderful hours. We both turned around and giggled. We took our shower. I led him to the door once he was dressed. We kissed each other goodbye and I promised to call him later on during the day.

Manny became my booty call of all booty calls. I gave dude a key to my apartment for him to let himself in after midnight on the weekends. He would come into my apartment when I was asleep and just lay the pipe on me. I mean really, do you know what it feels like to have dude come in while you are dead sleep and start to eat your pussy? Well it was addicting. With Manny I could let my inhibitions go. But I didn't see a future with him. I knew at some point we would have to approach this 'us' subject because he started to ask about 'us'. I sure as hell didn't want there to be an 'us'.

I made sure he always left, never spending the night and none of that cuddling shit. I would just let him come in and lay the pipe as good as it was. I just couldn't become his girl.

Me, a drug dealer's girl yeah I don't think so.

When the subject was brought up, I used to tell dude, "you need to leave and while you're at it take the garbage with you." Eventually I had to take my key back from him and had to go through some serious withdrawals. Manny was hard to shake. The sex was incredible. I had to do a couple of emergency calls and visits as well. It was a process but I managed because, the L word came up a couple of times and I knew for me it was LUST and not LOVE.

Movie

Monica Martinez

Sharon and Carlos were newlyweds and had been married for less than a year. Sharon was twenty four, Carlos thirty eight; it was the first marriage for both of them. An unlikely couple, Sharon a Kingston, Jamaica native was 5'9 and weighed 150 lbs. She had perky 36 C breasts, a small waist and wide hips. Carlos on the other hand was 5'6 weighed about 175 pounds he was thick and stocky. However, he was packing in the member area. Carlos was not born with good looks so he knew he would have to work hard to get the kind of money that warranted attention from women. His eyes were a rare colour gray, he had a gap in his front teeth and his lips were too small for his face. His parents were of White and Cuban decent. He worked his way up through the music industry for years and now he was a well known producer. Women would only use Carlos for two things, his money and his thick pipe. Other than that they really didn't want to be caught in public with him.

They met while he went on vacation in Jamaica about a year ago. Sharon was a receptionist at the front desk of the hotel he was staying at. When Carlos eyes fell on the dark beauty, the first thing he noticed was her full lips and her white teeth. He looked Sharon in her green eyes and instantly fell into a trance. She was beautiful; he couldn't help but stare at her.

Sharon said, "Excuse me sir, do you want to check in?"

It took Carlos a few seconds to realize she was talking to him. Carlos eventually had her agree to go out with him and show him the town. During his entire two week stay in Jamaica he spent every day taking her out to lunch and having her show him the island.

She was young and full of energy; just what he needed in his life. Sharon would take him all over, even to the little hole in the wall clubs and she'd make sure he returned home safely. Sharon knew Carlos was a man of wealth but wasn't familiar with his line of work. Unlike American women,

Sharon wasn't materialistic. Carlos loved that about her. She wasn't concerned about his looks, she enjoyed him for him. He knew she was something special. The night before Carlos was scheduled to leave, he had taken Sharon out shopping and they had dinner in his hotel room. Sharon wanted to send him on his way a very happy man. She also wanted to showcase just how Jamaican women were hot in the bed with the whining and grinding. When Carlos went to take a shower, Sharon slithered on his bed and placed an x-rated movie in the DVD player.

He came out of the shower to find Sharon naked on his bed. Her silhouette was beautiful as she presented herself against the white sheets. He noticed the movie playing.

"You want some of this?" He asked.

She laughed, "Mi a gwon show yu wat Jamaican women work wit."

A really hot scene showed, where the woman goes to her lover's job. They were kissing. He lifted her ass on his desk, parted her legs and started to taste her. The woman was arched, enjoying the feelings her lover was providing. This turned Sharon on. She motioned for Carlos to come to the bed. He did immediately. He put his hand on her thigh and started to caress her. Sharon started to feel herself get wet. Carlos's hand slid to her sweetness, touching her wet spot with his stubby fingers.

Sharon was moaning with the movie in the background, his fingers were moving around in circles on her clit.

The woman in the movie got on her knees to give her lover a nice oral job. Sharon turned to Carlos, kissed him with such intensity and lust. The movie was driving her crazy. She whispered in his ear "Mi wan fi fuck yu."

Carlos leaned her back and pulled her to the edge of the bed. He got on his knees. He took her in his mouth. He licked her sweet treasure softly at first, teasing her. Sharon closed her eyes. She had never experienced oral on her before. Most men in Jamaica thought it was dirty. Sharon started to breathe very hard as Carlos dashed his tongue up and down her inner lips across her gem. She started to move her hips as if she were dancing reggae. Carlos let her whine her pussy against his mouth as he took in her tasty juices.

Sharon moved her hips faster grinding against his tongue pushing his head deeper into her pussy. Carlos grunted as he watched his Jamaican beauty move with such gracefulness. He wanted to bring her to pleasure. Sharon's body started to quiver beyond control. She screamed. Carlos continued to lick her; he moved his tongue down to Sharon's ass. He dashed his tongue back and forth across her entrance. He ate her ass. Sharon screamed even louder. She held onto the bed pulling the sheets completely off. Carlos was pleased he made her cum. He got off of his knees and went to lie next to Sharon on the bed. He kissed her passionately. Sharon's very essence smelled like fruit juice. She kissed him sharing her flavor.

The man in the x-rated movie still had his lover on his desk. He entered her from behind while fondling her breasts.

Sharon got on all fours and told Carlos "Come tik it nah…"

Carlos wanted to enter her back door. His dick was hard and wet from the excitement. He entered slowly spreading Sharon's ass cheeks apart. She began to moan, began whining her hips again. Sharon wanted to get all of him inside of her hidden quarter pleasure. Carlos got really bold and said. "Beg for it."

Sharon begged, "Give mi yu big hood, mi wan it."

He continued to thrust harder and deeper.

Sharon whimpered, "It good, it good…" Over and over again, like it was a chorus of a song.

She started to bounce her ass harder onto his big dick. He took his hand and reached to play with her sweetness. Carlos couldn't take it anymore because her ass was tight.

He started to grunt very loudly. He went deeper filling her hidden quarter pleasure with his rod. He ejaculated inside of her with sweat pouring down him. He was drenched as he continued to pump inside of her ass while kissing the back of her neck.

After it was all over, Carlos whispered in her ear, "Come back to the states with me and be my wife."

Sharon was silent.

The two of them continued to fuck throughout the night. Sharon had given him all she had and they finished about three in the morning. Carlos was sprung and he knew he was taking her back home. Carlos stayed in Jamaica until Sharon was able to get her visa. He brought her to the States and made her his wife just as he promised.

Laundromat Excitement

Monica Martinez

$\mathcal{M}$ercedes walked into the twenty-four hour Laundromat at midnight. She figured she was going to be the only one doing laundry. Her life was hectic. She worked all day as a secretary. At night she was a waitress at a strip club. And she was going to school in between.

She went straight to the laundry from her night job, wearing boy shorts and a tiny top which showed off cleavage. When she entered the Laundromat just as she figured, she was the only one. She began separating her clothes, dividing the whites from the darks and making another pile for her towels.

She heard the doors to the Laundromat open. She turned to see who was coming in. In walked Elena, a beautiful Columbian girl. She had an olive tone to her skin. Black hair which fell to her shoulders and her eyes were blue. She had high cheek bones and her curves resembled Selma Hayek. She sashayed into the laundry and smiled at Mercedes.

Elena took at look at Mercedes and said, "Hello."

Mercedes greeted her with a pleasant smile. She was happy to see it was a woman and not a man. Men would always come on to her in the strip club, thinking she was one of the dancers. That turned her off, even when she was off work. She continued to separate her laundry while Elena brought her clothes closer to Mercedes.

Elena started a conversation asking Mercedes, "If you don't mind me asking, why you dressed like that coming to the Laundromat?"

Mercedes giggled and replied, "Girl, I work at a strip club, as a waitress in Mount Vernon."

"Oh," Elena asked. "What's the name of the club?"

"Rachel's Diamond"

"Oh, yes, I know of it."

"Are you a frequent visitor?" Mercedes asked with a laugh.

Elena chuckled, "No. I'm not a frequent visitor. I've been there a few times in the past."

Elena took notice, Mercedes wasn't wearing a bra and her nipples were erect. She could clearly see the outline of her nipples. Mercedes moved her eyes to see exactly what Elena was staring at.

Elena diverted her eyes in embarrassment.

Mercedes didn't mind getting attention from a woman. It came with the territory where she worked. And besides, she has already experienced a threesome before but never a one on one with a female. Elena was very attractive with her curvaceous body. She introduced herself "I'm Mercedes."

Elena said, "It's a pleasure to meet you, Mercedes. I'm Elena."

"Pleasure's all mine." Mercedes responded then commented on Elena's eyes. She said "You have the most beautiful blue eyes I'd ever seen." "Thanks." Elena said smiling.

She watched Mercedes bend down to put more clothes into the washing machine. Mercedes had sex appeal. She was working the non-existent outfit she had on. Mercedes was a 5'5, 125 lbs, Boricua with the hips and ass to proclaim the title. She had thick curly hair which came to the middle of her back. Mercedes stood, grabbed a scrunchy and put her hair into a pony tail.

"You are very pretty" Elena told Mercedes out of the blue.

Mercedes blushed. "You are very attractive yourself."

"Mercedes, do you do your laundry here often, at this time of the night I mean?"

"For the most part, I have such a busy schedule with work, during the day, school and this part-time job at night."

Elena said, "Wow, sounds like you got your schedule full. I just moved into the area not long ago. I find it easier to come at night. During the day it is way to busy and crowded with people."

Mercedes shook her head in agreement. Elena took a quick glance at Mercedes's body again.

She told Mercedes, "You're quite bold to come here dressed in such a revealing outfit."

Mercedes responded, "I figured no-one would be here. And besides, I don't have any clean clothes." The two women laughed.

Elena's pussy was throbbing, she was attracted to Mercedes. She wasn't sure if Mercedes was into women. Elena figured she'd take her chances and flirt some more.

"May I ask you something personal?"

Mercedes shook her head, yes.

"Are your breasts real, they look way to perfectly round."

Mercedes laughed. "Nope, I had them done about three years ago. Me and my home-girl took a trip to Brazil, got them for three thousand dollars."

"Well, damn, the doctor did a wonderful job. They are beautiful." Mercedes looked down at her breasts. She cupped them with her palms. "Yeah, he did. You can't even tell where he cut me."

"No...?" Elena said with curiosity. "Why's that?"

Mercedes added, "My nipples are brown and they don't even feel fake. I massaged them like the doctor told me to do every night for six months after the surgery."

She moved closer to Elena, "Touch," Mercedes suggested.

Elena was pleased. "Can I? I mean, if you don't mind."

"I wouldn't have suggested if I didn't mind."

Elena cupped Mercedes breasts into her hand and began massaging them softly.

Elena's touch sent a rush of excitement through Mercedes. Her pussy became wet instantly. Elena looked into Mercedes black eyes.

"Your breasts are nice, I like them."

Elena moved her fingers around in circles on Mercedes's nipples. Mercedes didn't stop her. Elena unbuttoned her little blouse and let her breasts go free. Elena moved her mouth to Mercedes bare breasts, started to kiss them softly. Elena's tongue was long, she teased Mercedes with it flickering it back and forth between breasts.

Mercedes moaned.

Elena moved down toward her belly, licking her all the way down to her belly button. She moved back to her breasts, Mercedes tasted like honeysuckle. Mercedes body was trembling, her knees visibly shaking.

Elena asked, "Are you nervous? Do you want me to stop?"

Mercedes looked around the Laundromat. They were the only ones inside. "Don't stop," She whispered in spite of the emptiness. "Please continue doing what you are doing."

"Have you ever been with a woman before?" Elena inquired.

"Not really," Mercedes answered. She knew that wasn't completely the truth. It was, sort of the truth. She reiterated. "I was in a threesome but I didn't get with the girl. I just got with the girl's husband. She watched him fuck me."

Elena frowned and then smiled. "Then it wasn't a real threesome."

Elena pushed her tongue into Mercedes's mouth. Both their breaths were fresh and clean. Mercedes closed her eyes and kissed Elena back like she'd tongued a woman a thousand times. She had never felt something so sensual in her life.

Elena's caressed Mercedes seductively; she lifted Mercedes onto a washing machine. The machine was just about to go into rinse cycle. Elena pushed Mercedes's boy shorts to the side and began working her tongue up and down Mercedes's crevices. Mercedes leaned enjoying the feeling Elena was providing. She moaned as Elena's long tongue flickered around her hard gem. Elena moved her tongue deep into her brown hole and used her lips, sucking her nectar. Placing a finger inside of her wetness she arched Mercedes back and fingered fucked her while the machine went full blast into the rinse cycle. Between the vibration of the machine and the sensations of Elena's fingers, Mercedes felt like she was being fucked with a dick.

She watched Elena's finger move in and out of her pussy and the machine bounced. Mercedes felt her eruption on the way as Elena moved her tongued harder onto her clit.

Mercedes yelled, "I'm gonna cum."

Elena pushed deeper into her pussy hitting her g-spot. Then she felt the gush come down onto her fingers. Elena moaned and revisited the bottom of Mercedes's pussy with her tongue taking the liquid into her mouth.

Mercedes legs were trembling. She felt like she had just run a marathon, she couldn't move. The washing machine stopped. Elena was pleased to see Mercedes had enjoyed herself. She helped Mercedes down from the washing machine. Mercedes legs caved in. Elena grabbed her quickly before she fell completely to the floor.

Mercedes said, "Damn," She was looking at Elena with dreamy eyes. "You made me weak at the knees."

They both chuckled. She helped Mercedes fix her clothes. They shared another kiss when the buzzer of the machine startled them. Then two women who looked like sisters entered the Laundromat.

Elena put her clothes into a cart and gave Mercedes her phone number. She told her to keep in touch. Mercedes gladly accepted with a satisfied smile on her face. The two women said goodbye to each other.

Mercedes knew she would call Elena sooner than later.

Ecstacy
Monica Martinez

$\mathcal{I}$ planned an evening of sex for my man whom I've been with for two years. I made reservations at the Marriott Marque Hotel in NYC for his birthday. I arrived there before he did and set up the room. He was scheduled to meet me at 9:00 p.m. The room was softly lit with pheromone candles.

When he came in, I told him to sit down. I licked my lips and got into dirty girl mode. It was about pleasing him this weekend. I was a lady by day and his freak by night. I am everything that represents a Latina, *shit* I stand 4'11 and weight about 110 lbs, long dark hair. My eyes are brown and I have a body that could make any man go crazy. My measurements are 34C 23 and 40 inch hips, which means *"Phat ass."*

Enrique was only able to see the silhouette of my body. He reached out because he wanted to touch me. I told him no and to just sit back and watch. I did a show for him.

I sat on the chair across from him, fully clothed. I wore a black fitted dress with red pumps. I began to undress seductively leaving my panties, bra and heels on. Enrique eyes widened as I opened my legs taking my panties bunching them up like dental floss inside of my 'girl'. I started to rub and grind hard against my 'valley'. My 'phatty girl' overlapped onto my lace panties, swollen and throbbing. I knew Enrique wanted me just from seeing the bulge in his pants. He was packing and there was no denying that.

Shit, what else could I ask for? He had all the qualities I wanted in a man. He was strong, a good provider, smart and damn good looking at that. My man is 5'8 slim build, jet black hair which he keeps in a fade. His eyes are hazel and he has long fingers and big feet, which ultimately means big dick. He pulled his eight inch thick rod out of his pants and began to stroke his shaft while watching me. I'm not even gonna lie, I love when he does that. I licked my lips and took my finger, started rubbing my clitoris. I brought my finger to my mouth to taste my essence, all the while letting out a slight gasp. I wanted him. I motioned for him to come over.

He stood in front of me, proceeded to get down on his knees. I put my legs onto his shoulders when he started licking me with my panties still on. He ripped them off of me and I screamed "Aye...."

He rotated his tongue to explore every nook and cranny of my walls. I held the arms of the chair tighter begging for more, "Give me more Papi" I told him, pushing my 'girl' deeper onto his tongue. His licks became more intense. I cried out and pulled onto his hair. He pushed my legs further apart to stick his tongue deeper inside of me. He took his time, not rushing, making it so pleasurable, "I'm there baby I'm about to explode" I moaned and my body started to tremble as I released into his mouth...

He stood and inserted his hardness inside me, began grinding slowly. We shared a passionate kiss as he whispered in my ear about how good and tight I felt inside. My juices creamed down onto his shaft.

I whimpered "Papi you make me feel good." He kissed my neck pushing deeper inside of me. I scratched and dug my nails into his back while biting his chest, leaving love marks. We started going at it faster, panting and moaning. I screamed "Give me that hard cock. Dame Papi" I screamed.

He liked the way my sweetness was contracting onto his hot stiff rod. He got aroused because he started to move faster wanting to bring pleasure to himself. I said to him "I want to feel the hot splash up against my wet walls." I needed to feel his heat inside of me. He grunted as he came to pleasure and filled up my sweetness.

We continued making love till our bodies couldn't take it anymore. It was ten thirty when we were done. I rested on his chest because I knew we weren't finished just yet...

The weekend was going to prove to be a great one for us. I had so many other treats in store for him. Enrique would be completely satisfied for his birthday. I planned it to be a birthday he would continue to talk about well into our old age.

He turned to me and said "Mami this is the best birthday gift I ever received." I smiled because in two hours the strippers were going to arrive and the party would just begin.

Besos *(kisses)*

Posh Party

Monica Martinez

Featured in Posh Magazine 2007

Once again, it was time for the biggest party of the year. We never arrive together because of our conflicting time schedules. The rule was, as soon as you walked in, immediately search for the others. It was really fun that way.

When I walked into the party I realize it's the same as always, very exciting. It's an elegant event, very classy. The music playing heightened the night's expectations even more. I was really looking for one person in particular, you. I'm feeling really sexy and the mood of the party is doing something to me. I spot you at the bar, Damn I can't wait to get a lick, I think to myself. I moisten my lips and start to move towards you. I come behind you.

I whisper in your ear, "Is this seat taken," as my hands reach around and brush against your nature.

You turn and smile deciding to play my game.

I buy you a drink and offer my new name to you. We play awhile back and forth with little sexy flirts. I want you. I really need you now. My sweetness is craving your touch. I wonder if we can sneak away, even for just a moment. I take your hand and request for you to follow me. I saw a room earlier that was unoccupied where everyone had put their jackets. I lead you to the room. The lights are off. Once we enter I push you against the wall and kiss you. My kiss is so powerful, because I'm so hungry for you. Biting your bottom lip, thrusting my tongue into your mouth, I take my right hand reaching for your nature rubbing on it. The thought of people mingling in the next room has you hard, the mere thought of having someone walk in on us is driving you crazy.

I take your 'big boy' out and get on my knees. I place you into my mouth, softly at first. You moan with pleasure, as I tease you with little licks. Then I take you completely in my mouth.

You start to thrust inside with hard strokes as you hold onto the back of my head. Exploring the back of my throat I can feel you getting more aroused as you grow more and more in my mouth. It's exciting me, making me moist. You can't take it anymore. You take me off my knees and push me against the door. You lift my dress. You slide my panties to the side without a struggle, so glad I didn't wear boy shorts today. As you slide into my sweetness slowly, my knees buckle, I explode as you enter me. My nectar is dripping down onto your shaft while you continue stroking me.

You are sucking on my neck and your right hand is caressing my nipples through my dress. I'm moaning. I really want to scream because of the pleasures you are giving me. Knowing it may signal someone to the room you cover my moan with your left hand. I bite onto your hand as I try not to scream. You continue to thrust deeper and harder into my love canal. I love the feeling of you inside of me. We hear someone coming towards the room you start to move faster because you want to attain pure gratification before they enter. I arch my back for you to go deeper into my sweetness. You grunt a bit too loud. I can feel you are near your peak. I move my hips along with your motion. I whisper in your ear, I want to feel your hot juices fill my insides.

You start to thrust faster into me. I enjoy the fact someone is approaching. Your breathing becomes more of a pant. I reach to caress and tease your sac with my fingernails. I know how much this turns you on when I do this. I want to bring you to an intense pleasure. I feel a rush of excitement just as the door knob turns. You release your hot splash into me and it splatters against my wet walls. Our body's tremble in unison as we both reached an intensified orgasm.

My pink pearl is hard from all of the excitement. As I feel our juices start coming down my leg, I shiver with more pleasure. The door opens and the lights go on, a couple enters the room. We start to adjust ourselves, as we giggle. I do believe we have just been caught at our Posh Party or shall we say our own Tantalizing Party.

I feel like a misbehaving teenager and what an intense feeling it is. We proceed to leave the room and go back to the main event to join the party. We hold hands and order some more drinks.

Let's get this party started we say as we head to the dance floor. We know we will continue our love making session when we "arrive" home. Or better still, who knows, maybe we'll take our chances again here?

Lipstick

Monica Martinez

They say only a woman can truly satisfy another.

I've gotten to the point in my life where I'm done with the game playing. Men are the biggest players and commitment phobia people I've ever met in my life. I can't deal anymore. I'm an independent woman who has her shit together. Most are intimidated by it, which is unreal to me. Who wouldn't want a smart, beautiful woman by their side? I've lost all interest in men, can't tell you when it happened though.

I remember being at work, Evelyn walked in with a black sleeveless dress. It fitted her body to the *T*. I looked her over with complete lust in my eyes. She was beautiful from head to toe. She was my secretary. I normally wouldn't start a conversation with her outside of work. I found myself dripping in my panties every time she came into my office to take notes or to ask me a simple question. I knew she was into women word around the office was, she was a lesbian.

She was on her way out when I called her back in.

"Evelyn" I called.

She turned. Her green eyes pierced through my soul. I remember all the blood rushing to my face when she looked at me. She licked her lips.

"Yes Jessica?"

"Can you bring me the latest stats on my figures?" I asked.

It was already five in the evening.

"Do you want the stats now?"

I told her if she was rushing she could get them to me first thing Monday morning.

Her response was, "No. I'm not rushing. Actually I can run them for you now."

I was pleased she said yes. Just maybe I would gather the nerves and ask her to join me for dinner. After all it was a Friday night; I didn't have any plans as usual. Evelyn came back in my office about an hour and a half later with the stats. I thanked her.

She asked if I needed anything else. I looked her over. She was hot. She stood 5' and she couldn't weigh no more than 125 lbs. She had jet black hair against her olive tone. She was exotic looking, her lips were full, and she had a mole above her lip on the left side. She had nice size breast if I had to guess she was a 34b. She possessed a small waist and a nice plump booty. She was a lipstick lesbian, very girly. I had never seen her dress like a dyke. She wore very little make-up and lip gloss. Her nails were always cut short but neat. She wore only clear polish.

"Jessica, did you need anything else?" She asked.

I stuttered a response. I don't know where my mind went. I must have been daydreaming. "I'm... sorry... Evelyn, actually I'm good. I was wondering if you were hungry. Maybe we could get a bite to eat? My treat, of course..."

Evelyn smiled and agreed to dinner with me.

I called City Crab to see if we could make a quick reservation as I didn't want to wait. It was perfect. They would have a table for two at seven thirty.

We walked over to the restaurant since we still had some time on our hands. We chatted all the way there. Evelyn was curious as to why I was alone and not dating. I smiled when she asked.

"Well most men seem to have a problem with a powerful woman. They can't seem to be able to deal with the fact I'm making over three figures and handling my business. They call me an Alpha female."

We both laughed together.

"I'm impressed. Such a beautiful woman as your self is on point. We don't have too many Latina's up there. You are my inspiration. I admire you."

I blushed when she said these things because I saw her eyes graze over my body. Evelyn was twenty five. However, she was more mature than any other twenty five year old I've ever met. She seemed to have an old soul about her. As beautiful as she was you could see she lived with pain in her eyes. I thanked her for the compliment.

We arrived at City Crab and headed over to the bar. I ordered a much needed glass of wine. Evelyn ordered a Long island ice-tea. I turned to her.

"Long Island Ice-tea huh, I see you're starting the weekend off just right."

She looked at me with a smile. "Damn right! We are

going to start this weekend off the right way. After dinner you are going to come out with me to a club."

I chuckled. "Nena, I don't do the club scene any more. Those days are over for me."

"Well you have never been to this type of club."

I smiled, worded "Exactly," I thought about things and said, "Where do you plan on taking me?"

She said, "I plan on taking you to a place where no one is intimidated by such a powerful woman."

The minute it left her lips I felt myself drip. She was getting me excited. She was flirting with me and I was enjoying it.

We talked some more at dinner. She told me how she knew she was a lesbian. She always thought she was different from the other girls. They were into boys and she was more interested in them. Not to mention how she lost her virginity. It was painful to hear it was her uncle who had taken it away. He molested her. After that, she had never wanted anything to do with a man, ever again. Her parents had found out when she got pregnant at the age of eleven. She never gave birth. She had a miscarriage. Her parents had the uncle put away in jail. Then they sent her to Puerto Rico to be with her grandmother.

She came back to New York to go to college where she

was majoring in Psychology. Evelyn wanted to give back to little girls who had gone through similar situations as her. I commended her for being strong and being able to live through such a horrible childhood.

She smiled appreciating my concern. "I'm in a good place in my life. My parents made sure to give me tons of love and protect me. I just live a life admiring women and loving their beauty."

I gave her a grin then waved the waiter over. We ordered our dessert.

We were done with dinner at nine thirty. Since, I had been enjoying her conversation as well as her company. She said it was still too early to hit the club. Seeing as I lived in the city, I offered her to chill with me at my place until it was time for us to go. She had convinced me to go with her. I must say I was actually looking forward to it.

We got to my apartment on the upper west side within twenty minutes. Once inside my adobe, I poured us two glasses of white wine. We sat on the sofa. Evelyn looked around my apartment.

"You got a nice pad" she told me.

I thanked her for the compliment and told her to walk

around and check it out. She rose from where she was sitting and asked me to show her around. I told her it would be my pleasure.

I showed her my home office, guest bedroom, the kitchen and the two bathrooms. We found ourselves in the Master bedroom where I have an adjoining bathroom. The bathroom has marble all over, glass enclosed shower and an old fashion bathtub.

She motioned to my king sized bed and asked if she could sit.

"Of course," I answered.

"You're bed is so comfortable." She told me after she sat.

I stood in the doorway with a smile admiring her beautifully toned legs. I was feeling her because she possessed qualities similar to mine. She was beautiful had sex appeal which was a rare combo in women. I felt my pussy pulsating hungry for her touch.

"Jessica, sit with me on your bed."

I moved to my bed, took my shoes off before I sat next to her.

She asked if I had ever been with women before.

My response: "No, never in my thirty years."

She smiled "What if I told you there are different types of lesbians?" I just looked at her with wide eyes and listened. "There are the lesbians that look like guys who don't let you touch them, because they want to be men. There are lesbians who are hot, such as my self," she let out a chuckle before she continued, "Who can make you never want to go back to a man. We can make you feel better than any man ever could."

I smiled at her words. "Then I would be schooled. You have just taught me something."

We laughed together.

It was at that moment Evelyn leaned in and kissed me.

I had never experienced something so sensual. Her breath was so inviting. I was hungry for her. She moved me to lay flat on the bed and maneuvered her body on top of mine while she continued to kiss me. It was a very tender kiss. I've never felt the kind in my life till then. Her hands went underneath me and on my ass. She groped me but it was done tastefully.

She pulled away, softly worded "Jessica, are you okay?"

I shook my head, yes. I didn't want her to stop. The feelings were surreal and my panties were drenched. She moved down to my neck, her hands began to unbutton my shirt. She pulled me from the bed to unzip my skirt. I stepped out of my skirt. We locked eyes…

She was beautiful. My body screamed for her touch.

She asked for me lay on the bed. She wanted me to relax. I tried to catch my breath. I didn't know what to expect from her.

She told me, "Close your eyes and enjoy the ride."

I closed my eyes. I wanted her to make love to me.

Could she make love to me better than a man? I wondered.

She grabbed the lotion off of my dresser, started at my feet and slowly moved her way to my calves. Her touch was soft and firm. I felt light-headed as she massaged my inner thighs. I let out a soft moan. She skipped over my 'prize' and worked her way to my belly button where she circled it with her finger tips. Her touch brought goose-bumps through-out my body. The feelings she was providing were beyond what my imagination thought it would be.

She managed to get her hands behind my bra and unclasped it, freeing my 36 C's.

She moaned a very audible, "Mmmmm. Jessica you are beautiful."

She kissed on my neck softly. She sucked on my neck and began biting me tenderly. She moved down towards my breasts. She started to massage them one by one. She brought my nipples to her mouth. I came instantly as she sucked on them.

"Aye Mami, it feels good. Please don't stop" I whispered.

Evelyn moved from my breast to the center of my belly, once again circling my belly button but with her tongue this time. I arched my head back to take the feelings in. She worked her way even further down, to my thongs, rubbing her hands on my slits. My legs were shaking. I felt as if I were going to explode once again.

"Dame mas!" I screamed.

She continued to rub her hand on my panties pushing them up like dental floss, teasing my clit. She rubbed on my clit with her thumb as she pushed my thong aside. I was losing it. The rush of my nectar leaked at a steady pace. She was enjoying the fact that she was making me cum so much in such a short period of time.

She moved her head in between my legs and her hair caressed my body and it sent a rush of excitement through me. I screamed her name as she went in for my clit sucking while rubbing against my second set of lips. They were pulsating. I felt all the blood rush to that part of my body.

I grabbed at my comforter and pulled at it.

My body began jerk almost violently. She slid her tongue from my clit to my lips, down to my tunnel. Within minutes the tidal wave had come shooting into her mouth.

She drank all of my succulent juices gulping and moaning. She placed two fingers into my wet pussy inching them to my g-spot, making my body jerk anew. With her free hand she held onto my stomach and felt me contract as she made me cum even harder than I had before.

My heart was racing and she wasn't even done with me yet. I had to look to see if she was using something to penetrate me. It actually felt as if I were being fucked by a man with a nice size dick. Damn, she was twisting me out...

I grabbed at her head and pushed her face deeper in to my pussy. She loved it. She began to move her fingers faster and deeper inside of me.

"Evelyn...!" I screamed.

In spite of my protest she didn't stop. She moved her tongue along with the rhythm of her fingers and made me orgasm again. My body felt as if there was no more to come out of me. I was dripping in sweat and felt as if I ran a marathon but there was no stopping her. Just when I didn't think I had anymore inside of me, she was going to prove me wrong.

Evelyn turned me around, positioned me on all fours and pulled my panties off. I couldn't imagine what else she had in store for me. She wrapped my hair around her arm and kissed the back of my neck. She moved down my entire spine with her tongue. My body began to tingle...

She was at the small of my back when she released my hair from her hands and grabbed my ass cheeks apart. She thrust her tongue down the crack into my backdoor. I almost collapsed as my arms gave way. I came instantly from both ends. She moved her fingers back inside of my wet walls while she continued to eat my ass out.

"Oh... my... goodness...!" I screamed.

She made me cum three more times.

I fell to my bed exhausted. She had made love to me for over two hours. She was right about making me feel better than any man could. I turned to her and smiled. Evelyn was still dressed. I begged for her to come lay in the bed with me naked. She shrugged her shoulders in uncertainty.

"Are you sure?" She asked.

"Please spend the night with me."

Evelyn lifted her dress over her body. She had nothing underneath.

She was beautiful from head to toe.

Evelyn and I cuddled till we fell asleep.

She taught me how to make love to a woman. I was a good student because now we are living together as partners. Evelyn received her degree and is working for the city, helping children who've been molested deal with the pain. As for me, I'm in a wonderful place in my life. She proved to me the saying; only a woman can truly satisfy another.

Pay Back
Monica Martinez

Shanice and Keith had been together for six years. The first two were amazing she was everything to him and vice versa. In their third year together he started cheating with anything that passed his way and gave him the opportunity. He would use a bullshit excuse as the reason why he cheated. Keith would tell women "Me and my wife don't have sex. I'm just with her cuz of our daughter." Shanice always thought the women were dumb because if a guy is married; and he sleeps in the bed with the same person on a regular they are definitely having sex.

She thought their sex life was good until she found out

he was having affairs. Although the women meant nothing because the minute she found out about the chick, Keith would drop them like a bad habit. Shanice continued to play the good wife and stand by her man. She followed what she was taught at a young age, watching all the women in her life do the same exact thing. It wasn't until one day; she bumped into an old boyfriend of hers. Back in the day she loved this guy. He broke her heart because she was a virgin and wasn't giving up the sex. How time flies and things changed, but all for the good he didn't change a bit. Fine as ever when she bumped into him. Shanice on the other hand was all giddy and shy. She was truly acting like a school girl with her crush all over again.

Dave was 5'9 Puerto Rican about 165 lbs, all muscles. He was dark skinned. His lips always drove her crazy. Dave was the first person to teach her how to kiss. When they bumped into each other they talked for a good deal of time. He flirted with her. This made Shanice automatically weak at her knees and drip. Eventually he asked her if she was happy. Shanice didn't know how to respond but she immediately said no. "Damn," He said. "I thought you would be happy."

Shanice shook her head no and asked Dave if he was married.

He responded, "Naw I just live with my son's mother." He said he and his girl were on good terms. Being a man he couldn't resist the temptation and asked Shanice for her number.

She provided him with her beeper and work number. They agreed to definitely keep in touch. He went to kiss her goodbye on the cheek; she turned for him to kiss her lips. She wanted to feel his sexy ass lips once again. Besides, no one has ever replaced his kiss not even Keith. They kissed with what felt like eternity and her 'bad girl' got even wetter. She wanted to make love to him right then and there. They said goodbye once again and went their separate ways.

Two days later Dave called her at her job and wanted to do lunch with her. Dave wanted to fuck her because he didn't get the chance when they were younger. They both played catch up and Shanice felt like there was no other place she would rather be. For a moment Shanice forgot she was a married woman.

During lunch, Dave leaned over and kissed her. He ran

his finger through her hair. It felt like heaven to Shanice. She had never been touched with such passion in years. She reciprocated the kiss. Dave told her, he had always and never stopped loving her. He apologized for the way they broke up back in the day. She laughed at him told him it was okay. They were young and it didn't matter especially since they were together at the moment. Dave agreed to meet Shanice after work. He had already secured a good lie for his girl. His brother was covering for him today. At exactly five o'clock he was there as promised to pick her up. He told her he would drive her home. They were in his car listening to music and talking about the good old times. How they used to meet at the arcade and hold hands. How she used to sneak out to go to the movies with him. How Shanice had to have her sister cover for her to meet with him.

Damn she thought to herself *I really want to fuck him.* There was no question in her mind. When they got to her apartment, she knew her husband wasn't gonna be home any time soon. It was Friday and he was a creature of habit. It was a rare event if he did show and not hang out instead. Shanice led Dave upstairs to the apartment the boldest move she ever made. As soon as they entered he turned her around closed the door and pulled her close to him.

He told her, "I want to make love to you."

They were kissing when her phone rang. The caller-Id showed it was Keith calling. She put her finger to her mouth for Dave to be quiet.

Keith was giving her another story about how he had to work late, again. This only meant he was probably on another date with one of his side chicks. It didn't matter to Shanice because payback was a bitch and Dave was already in their apartment. Shanice had already planned on fucking him regardless. *Shit if he can do it then so can I* she thought. You heard the song *A woman needs love*. Well shit Shanice needed some loving.

"Yeah okay," She said to Keith. "I'll see you later." When she hung the phone up, Dave hungrily kissed her. She pulled at his clothes to take them off. She wanted to explore this man. She had unfinished business with him. His body was amazing muscles everywhere. She ran her finger up and down his six pack licking her lips.

Shanice told him how much she loved his body. He took off her top and brought her nipples into his mouth. Shanice felt like she was dreaming, leaning her head back while moaning with pleasure. She felt his hard dick through his underwear. She couldn't wait till it was inside of her. Dave brought her to the couch and laid her down. He told her of how much he dreamed of this day and he wanted to please her. He took off her skirt and panties, leaning into her pussy licking around her lips making her squirm. Shanice shivered she wanted him badly. He took her clit into his mouth and sucked on her till she came hard. He sipped her juice and drank it like it was apple juice.

He removed his underwear, this was the first time she had seen his dick. For a minute Shanice was scared because it was so big. He told her not to worry and inserted his dick inside of her. He moved slowly till her pussy got adjusted to his big dick. They were kissing each other with a strong desire for one another. It was heavenly to be making love to him for the very first time. She always wondered what it would have been like. She begged Dave to give her all of him. He began to fuck her harder and he got more excited. His body started to jerk while he was pumping in her. He grunted and told her he was going to cum. He took his dick out of her and squirted his cum all over her stomach. Shanice rubbed his cum all over her stomach and breasts.

This excited him even more. He wasn't finished with her. He lifted her and carried her to the bedroom. He told her he wanted to fuck on 'their' bed. Shanice didn't stop him from taking her to the very bedroom she shared with her husband. For a moment she thought about it and remembered that, two weeks ago some chick called the house telling her what her fucking bedroom looked like. So obviously her husband had been bringing women there. So what was good for the goose was definitely good for the gander. Shanice got on all fours for him and started to play with her pussy as he watched. She motioned for him; she was ready to receive what he wanted to give her. He came closer to her slowly sliding his rod into her wet pussy. Shanice backed on his strong dick. She moved her ass against his stomach.

She screamed, "Fuck me, give me that dick…. give it to me."

He put his hands on her ass. He started pumping harder, faster and breathing heavy.

He eventually stopped, dropped to his knees. He took her pussy into his mouth. He was eating her out again; there was no stopping this man. Shanice couldn't take it because it was feeling so good. She came hard into his mouth. He moved back and pounced on her pussy and began fucking her harder. She wanted more. She begged for him to go deeper. He went deep, grabbing her hair asking if she liked it.

She replied, "I love it."

He smacked her on the ass.

Dave turned her around putting his cock in her mouth,

telling her, "Take that."

Shanice sucked on his dick something she rarely ever did for Keith. She wasn't with sucking his dick. She wasn't good at giving head but she sure as hell was going to try. She started to gag. Dave didn't care because it was feeling good...

Shanice's saliva was coming down from her mouth and getting on his balls. Dave was going nuts.

He pulled her to the edge of the bed and started to fuck her. He wanted to cum in her mouth he told her.

Shanice straddled him and started to ride his dick holding on to the headboard. She moved her hips and grinded on his dick while he played with her nipples. The two of them were drenched in sweat.

He murmured he was going to cum. Shanice quickly jumped off of his dick and got to her knees. He shot his nice hot cum in her mouth. She swallowed it and sucked till everything came out of him, something she hardly did for Keith, ever. To her Keith's cum tasted nasty. Besides Keith wasn't circumcised and had a smell to it. Just as she finished swallowing Dave's delicious cum, the phone rang again.

It was Keith and all she could do was smile. Keith informed her he wouldn't be getting in till Saturday morning.

Dave and Shanice took a hot shower where he fucked

her all over again. Her pussy was so sore by the time Dave left her. Shanice mellowed in their scent and rolled around the bed smiling. She knew she would have to clean the mess before Keith showed.

Shanice was putting on clean linens when she heard the keys in the door. *Oh my goodness* was all she could think. Keith had decided to come home after all. She hurried and took the sheets to the hamper and sprayed the room with air freshener.

Keith walked into the bedroom.

"Wow you are up late." Keith said in shock.

Shanice grinned. "Yeah, I wanted to see if you were really trying to spend the night out."

She really was nervous and thought for sure he was going to know she had someone in their bedroom. Keith didn't say a thing. All he did was undressed and went to sleep. She thought to herself *payback is a bitch...*

Dave and Shanice continued to have an affair until she left her husband Keith. Although Dave and Shanice never ended up together he was definitely good for her ego. Shanice loves him till this day and would drop whoever she was with to be with him. First loves are the hardest to get over.

Park, In the Dark

Monica Martinez

$\mathcal{M}$yra was involved in a relationship which wasn't fulfilling her needs. However she wasn't ready to walk away from the man she loved. She knew her man was fooling around with all the bullshit excuses he would give to her about working late at night. She met Todd at the gas station she frequented. She used to eye him whenever she saw him. They both used the gas station regularly. She was waiting for him to notice her and say something.

One morning she walked into the gas station's store to pay the cashier. Todd was on line. He touched her hand. "Excuse me if you want, you are more than welcome to skip ahead of me."

Myra smiled and said, "Thank you."

Todd was admiring her every curve and she knew it. It felt as if her whole entire back was burning with fire.

Myra stood 5'0, weighted 107 lbs, and was measured 32 C, 24, and 38. She was a Puerto Rican beauty. She had jet black hair that went down her back, which she loved to wear loose. Her eyes were very seductive. She was very sensual in the way she walked. She had beauty and sex appeal. He knew it was rare for a woman to posses both of these qualities. He had watched her for the longest time and was waiting for an opportunity to talk to her.

Todd watched her walk to her car and figured here it goes. He introduced himself as she pumped her gas. He gave her his number and told her he would love to take her to dinner some day.

They met for dinner about a week later. Myra thought Todd had a swagger about him. He definitely had her interest. It was a nice fall day a little brisk, after work Myra met Todd in the park. They were holding hands while walking. They sat down on the bench to watch the geese in the water. He leaned in to her, give her kiss. It was a nice innocent kiss.

Their lips had never met until that very moment. It was a peck but his kiss sent chills down her spine and made her quiver. Myra didn't want to seem anxious but she wanted another kiss something more lustful. Myra wanted him, she reached for another kiss. Their lips met once again. Myra thrust her tongue into his mouth. She wanted to explore his mouth to see if the feeling would be more intense than the peck he gave her earlier.

It was, she instantly became wet, and it was evident they shared sexual chemistry. He was at least a foot taller than her. Myra had to stand on her tip toes to give him kisses. He pulled her by the waist pushing his hard body against her. It felt as if a surge of electricity went through her. He pulled away from her and suggested they walk; otherwise, he wouldn't be accountable for his actions.

It began to get dark and a little chilly. They were enjoying one another's company and didn't mind one bit. Todd was 6' and 195, lbs, with a caramel complexion. He had brown eyes. His lips were semi full. Myra found him incredibly sexy. She turned around putting her arms around his neck, bringing him down for another kiss.

This time he lifted her into his arms. She felt the bulkiness from his jeans. She wanted him just as much as he wanted her. They were still in the park and in spite of the night and the chill, decided to sit again. He told her he was very attracted to her. The feeling was mutual, her sweetness began to throb. He stood in front of her and kneeled down with his hands on her knees. Myra took his hands, moved them up her thighs and gave him a seductive stare. She was wearing a skirt and high heel boots which came to her knees. He inched his hand closer to her heat. She had given him every indication she wanted him. His hand found itself resting in between her thighs.

"Your pussy is hot." He blurted.

She whispered, "She's hot for you."

He proceeded to rub her with his fingers. Myra moaned softly. He had found and began touching her clit.

He looked around to make sure there wasn't anyone around. Satisfied there wasn't, he lifted her skirt a little higher. He placed his head between her legs kissing her thighs. She edged him on for more. He got closer to her butterfly. Myra leaned back to bring her body closer to his mouth. She wanted to show him she wanted him there. Her man hadn't touched her in over two months. Todd moved her panties to the side and started to lick around her butterfly. He kissed the outer lips with tender kisses.

It was too much for her. She began to moan louder not caring they were in the park. He began to suck on her sweet butterfly sticking his tongue deep inside of her. She was wet beyond belief and enjoying the pleasure.

Todd lifted her legs onto his shoulders. Myra's body jerked. She covered her mouth to mute her moaning as she released in his mouth. She grabbed on tight to the park bench preventing herself from falling. She was biting on her lower lip. He took a finger and inserted it into her dripping pussy.

Myra took his finger slowly into her mouth sucked on it as if she was sucking a dick. He told Myra her juices were sweet and addicting.

She giggled. First he fixed her panties and then she rose off the bench. He pulled her closer into him. Todd asked her if she enjoyed herself.

"Very much so" she answered.

Myra told him she would like to take it to the next level, if possible.

He smiled. He told her he guaranteed their next encounter would be blissful.

He walked her to the car and gave her one more kiss before he sent her home. Myra drove off with a smile on her face and wondered when their next encounter would take place. The park was nice but...

"Can't wait to see him again," She worded to herself. "Can't wait..."

Cravings

Monica Martinez

$\mathcal{I}$ haven't seen him in a while. My body desires his very touch. I want his hands taking their time caressing my body. I yearn to feel his mouth kissing every part of me. I thirst to have his nature in my mouth bringing him to unknown pleasures. I'm hungry for him to taste my sweetness and make my body cry with pleasure. I'm in need for our bodies to become one, doing the same motions as we share our passion.

I would get on all fours for him. He could lick my back all the way down to my sweetness; where he should linger and relish my taste. I'd watch the reflection of us in the mirror as he takes me from behind and goes deep. Pleasure would be written all over his face. He'd utter the words I love to hear him say… "I love the way you feel."

I would reach my hands behind me just to touch him. He would pull my hair and kiss me with fervor.

He'd push his rod further into my tunnel, reach my g-spot and make me gush out warm fluid. I'd crave to feel the heat of his juice as he ejaculates into my sweetness or I would beg for him to burst his warm flavor into my inviting mouth. I desire to hear his moans, grabbing my head back while he's inside me. He asks me if I like it like that.

He turns me around and lays me on the bed hosting my legs on his shoulders, spreading my legs as far apart as they possibly could go. Then he is deeper inside of me. I'd yelp with excitement as his pole excavates my body. He hits my spot making my honeysuckle come down onto him. He'd stop and drink from the waterfall. He would move further up my body taking my nipples in his mouth, pulling at them until they are fully erect. He sucks on my neck, lies on the bed and pulls me on top of him. We would clasp our hands together as I bring him to ecstasy…

On the Bus

Monica Martinez

I woke up this morning later than normal. Damn-it, this is just not a good start to my morning. My boss will be all pissy. We have a meeting with one of our new authors and I'm going to be late. I knew I shouldn't have gone out with Tony and Mike last night. I jumped into the shower; threw on my Kenneth Cole suit with a burgundy button down shirt, and my Coach shoes. I called my boss; got his voice mail. Thank goodness, I sure as hell didn't want to hear his mouth. I checked the scheduled for the express bus and I had ten minutes to make it downstairs to get my ass on the bus. Hopefully we won't be in a shit load of traffic.

I don't even have time to stop for my morning coffee and this hang over isn't helping right now. I grabbed some Tylenol; headed out of my apartment down the block to the bus stop. Perfect I jogged and the bus just arrived, maybe my day will get better. I live in Fresh Meadows; Queens, I work at a publishing company in the city on Fifth Avenue. I'm an account manager, which means I got the lucky job of helping out with the new authors. I get to decide which author will be the new and up coming one we will help promote. I've been working at the company for six years and I can't complain I've been promoted three times already. My phone rings; I see my office number. Damn, not sure I should answer. I know it's my boss, shit...

"Hello, this is Jimmy."

"Jimmy Its Neil. Are you on your way? Our client called and asked us to move the meeting earlier than originally discussed."

"I'm just getting on the express bus as we speak. I should be there hopefully within the hour or sooner."

Neil said perfect see you then and severed the connection.

Damn, my day is getting better after all. That was my boss and he didn't even flip. Now that's what I'm talking about. I head to the back of the bus and take a seat. It's empty with the exception of a few people. Although it's only the second stop, my guess it will get crowded at some point. I put my iPod on to try to rest a little more, hopefully my headache goes away. I closed my eyes as we approach the third stop. I opened them about ten minutes later, because I felt as if someone was staring at me...

I looked directly at her. She quickly glanced away. She's fucking hot, a beauty on the bus. Just my luck, which means yeah my day is definitely getting better. She's Puerto Rican, I can tell. She has dark brown hair; it looks very long not sure where it stops. She's wearing a skirt suit, showing off her long sexy legs, with some nice high heel pumps. I directed my attention elsewhere and then look at her again. I caught her staring at me, again. She licked her lips in a seductive manner. Her lips are glossed and full. It is my turn to break my stare away. She is sexy as hell with that damn mini Ally McBeal type suit. I can't believe she is still staring me up and down, damn, I hope I meet the requirements.

I looked around to see what else she could be staring at and to see if anyone else is seeing what I'm seeing at this very moment. There aren't many people on the bus, probably about ten of us and they are way in the front of the bus. Wait a minute I think she's eye fucking me, holy shit. I look back at her and sure enough her eyes are focused on my crotch. Damn ain't this some shit; I've never been eye fucked before in all my twenty eight years, well, at least not to my knowledge. Man oh man my temperature is rising. I start to perspire. I know my shit is gonna get hard in a few minutes as she continues to stare at my manhood. Her eyes meet mines again, the loveliest eyes I've ever seen. They are gray and alluring.

With every look or glance she is seducing me and making me nervous. I'm slightly intimidated; this shit is bugging me out right now. She uncrossed her legs and then crossed them back with her hands on her knees. She looks me dead in my eyes as she undresses me. I watch as she lowered her eyes from my face to my chest as if she is unbuttoning my shirt. She moves back down to my crotch and leans forward to take her jacket off. She is wearing a white silk blouse; I can see her cream bra through it. She has a nice rack on her; my estimate is around a 34 b or c. Her nipples are erect and poking at me. She has straight up desire in her eyes.

She bites her lower lip as she looks me in face again, raising her eyebrows. I smile and she smiles back. She takes her hand and puts it behind her neck and does a sort of stretch. I watch as her tits lift, with erect nipples that yearn for my mouth. My dick is rising; I place my hands on top hoping I can stop it from growing. I'm grateful I'm in the corner by the window and no one is seated next to me. I open the window a little. She crossed her legs tighter, rubbing her thighs. I'm debating whether or not I should approach her. Wait a minute, I think she is having an orgasm as she closed her eyes and leans her head back. What the fuck? Is this really happening? She shivers; she opened her eyes again and looks at me with a grin. Fuck my pre-cum is seeping out to my underwear, my dick is throbbing. I want to fuck the shit out of her. The bus stops at 34th and 5th Avenue. She leaves her seat, smiles at me before she exits the bus.

She has a big ass on her and fuck, her body is sick. I shift in my seat and look out the window to get one last peek at her. I see her left hand, she is sporting a ring. She is taken. Well shit, I don't mind if she don't. I should have gotten her number, because I would have twisted her out at least once. I sure as hell would have taken her back to my crib and ate her pussy out till she screamed Hail Mother Fucking Mary. I would have made her cry out my name, yeah she would have been saying, "Jimmy…. Oh Jimmy, your cock is so good. Give me more…" Fuck my dick is hurting so bad right now and I can't do shit about it. I need to think about something else because my stop is next.

My phone rings. It's my boss. This definitely will bring my hard cock to a limp state.

"Hey…"

"Jimmy, where are you?"

"I'm exiting the bus as we speak boss. I'll be in the office in exactly ten minutes."

"The time is now nine forty five. We have fifteen minutes before the client comes in." Neil snapped and then severed the connection.

Perfect. I jog to the office.

I head upstairs and Monica has my coffee waiting as I step off the elevator. She gives me the scoop on the new author. I walk into our conference room and Neil is sitting by himself. He looks at me and says we have less then ten minutes to brief ourselves. The time is ten o'clock on the dot.

Monica opens the conference room and in walks our new author.

It just happens to be the same chick that was on the bus earlier.

Yeah, now that's exactly what's up. My day just got fucking better and the hangover headache is no longer.

Marine

Monica Martinez

He was a Marine. He travelled the world. He had game and the love of his life Jessica didn't know she was being played. He had been away for four months. Horacio had been Jessica's puppy love. They reconnected at the age of twenty three. They started what Jessica thought was a relationship. He told her he had since broken up with his daughter's mother when they started to see each other seven months ago; only Jessica didn't know he was still with the mother of his children. His baby's mother was expecting their third child any minute. Jessica waited for him; it was a hard and lonely four months for her. Their trip was scheduled for the day after he came home. Horacio was scheduled to come home in May. Jessica was so excited to be able to finally see and be with him.

She picked him up at JFK Airport. When she saw him she smiled showing her beautiful white teeth. She ran straight into his arms and gave him a big kiss. They held onto each other for what seemed like a very long time. He whispered in her ear how much he missed her. How he couldn't wait to get home to see her. They grabbed his luggage and jumped into her car headed towards her apartment in Queens Village.

Upon their arrival Jessica's roommate Janita was already home from work. They all chilled out and watch T.V. Jessica cooked Horacio a nice dinner; she made him rice, beans and pork chops with salad. It was around midnight when she started to pack for their mini vacation when he came into the room.

He just stood there and watched her. She hadn't notice he was standing there. Horacio cleared his throat and it startled her since she was concentrated on what she had been doing. She laughed and asked him what he was doing.

He said, "I was just admiring the view." He told her she

was beautiful, moved closer to her to give her a kiss.

His touch made all the hair on her arms stand and sent goose bumps all over her body. He whispered in her ear how much he loved her. He wanted to make love to Jessica. He closed the door to the room. R. Kelly's 'your body is calling' was playing.

Horacio was handsome he stood 5'11 weighed 210 lbs. He had dark brown eyes, full lips and was the complexion of dark mocha coffee. His body was fit because of his job.

Jessica was a white Latina with long blonde hair and brown eyes. She stood 4'9 and weighed 90 lbs. Her eyes were slanted like a Chinita. Horacio laid her down on the bed and kissed her very passionately. He touched her sweetness through her pajamas. Jessica was already wet. Her peach was throbbing and hot. He took his time removing her clothing. Jessica didn't have any panties on. He was surprised by this and moaned with pleasure. He was always pleased how well Jessica took care of her hygiene. He loved her wax job. She had a happy trail. He traced the trail with his tongue; it made Jessica shiver and moan. He proceeded to take her top off. Once that was gone he licked around her brown nipples. He worked his way back to her neck. He sucked and licked around it and brought his mouth to hers.

They began to tongue kiss. It made Jessica's pussy

ooze out nectar. She wanted him to enter her with his dick. He worked his way back down toward her stomach and continued giving her soft kisses, just enough to make her plead for more. He moved further down to the trail of her sweetness again. He requested her to pull herself closer to the head board. Once she did he took her dripping peach into his mouth, sucking softly. He wanted to savour the flavour of her essence. He took both of his hands spreading her second set of lips apart. Her nectar seemed endless and was trickling down her inner thighs. Horacio murmured how deliciously sweet she tasted. He didn't want to stop drinking. "Baby, I'm gonna suck you wet and fuck you dry."

He sucked on her clit till she couldn't take it anymore. She uttered a piercing cry and released all over his mouth. He picked up speed with his tongue dashing up and down, deep into her pussy.

He turned Jessica around and placed her on her stomach. There was an orange on the night table. He took the orange and squeezed all the juices down her back. Then he proceeded to lick it all off as it went down the back of her ass. The feelings were surreal to Jessica. She was in heaven. She never had anyone who made her feel so good. He got closer to her and grabbed her breasts into his hands from behind and began rubbing on her nipples. Whispering in her ear how he longed for her while he was away. Jessica begged him to take her. His pole was hard. She reached for it with a hand from behind. She got on her hands and knees on the bed. He entered her doggy style slowly grinding into her softly.

He asked if she was enjoying it.

Jessica whimpered, "Yes…" She was moaning with pleasure.

She started to push deeper onto his nature with her wet pussy. It got Horacio more aroused.

He removed his dick from her and asked her to lay flat on her stomach. He entered her again, went deeper inside her pussy, holding her ass apart. He was working so hard. He was panting.

He yelled out to Jessica, "Whose pussy is this?"

Jessica replied, "It's yours, Papi all yours."

She continued to beg for him to give her his hard nature and for him to bring out her sweet nectar. He went deeper, slowly giving her nice hard strokes in and out. He lifted her once again to all four limbs and cupped her breasts in his hands. He took his right hand and went straight for her clit. He was rubbing it as fast as he was fucking her. Their bodies were dripping with sweat. Jessica was sticky from the orange however the smell of it and their scent excited them even more. Jessica felt her entire body being emptied and filled over and over again by his dick. She began to shake. She was about to burst at any moment. She moved back to him, stretched her arms back grabbing his face, telling him to give it to her. She informed him she was about to cum. Horacio felt her release all over his cock.

He turned her around to her back facing him. He grabbed both breasts and put her nipples in his mouth and entered her again. He thrust into her open hole. His dick was growing inside of her. She felt it. She wanted him to cum bad. She needed to feel the heat of his juices inside her. That or she wanted them on her. Wherever he wanted to put them she was willing to take them.

"Papi give it to me harder, faster..." she cried. "I love you with all my heart. Give me all of you"

He continued with harder strokes, moving faster and deeper. He was grunting. He was at his peak.

"Baby...." he screamed.

Horacio came inside her pussy.

He was weak and dropped to the bed beside her. Jessica wanted to taste their scent. After he came inside her she turned to him, went lower and took his nature into her mouth, sucking whatever remaining juice he had. Jessica turned her attention to his sack and put his balls into her mouth. He squirmed with pleasure. She sucked on them one by one.

Jessica got on top of him. She rode his dick till it went completely limp.

He pulled her to his chest and whispered in her ear, "I love you."

She smiled and lay down on his chest. Horacio knew he impregnated Jessica that evening. Tomorrow they would continue their journey of love making on their mini vacation. She fell asleep in his arms.

Horacio waited until he knew for sure she was completely sleep and made his phone call to his children's mother. Horacio was in love with both women and didn't want to let either of them go. He knew Jessica would be heartbroken if she knew he was still with Lordes. Maybe when they came back from their trip he would tell her?

Whenever, Wherever, However.

Monica Martinez

Ernesto and I both worked for a cleaning company and our schedule was thrown off due to the night shift. We haven't been able to have sex for an entire week. This particular Friday night I threw on some fitted sweats pants and a wife beater *because like* who the fuck was gonna see me except Ernesto and other crew members. We arrived at one of the fast food chains we had a contract with. Soon I was bent over scrubbing the floor.

Ernesto turned around and said "Damn I've been

neglecting that; well not tonight."

I turned around and smiled, said. "We've been pre-occupied with work, so technically you haven't been neglecting anything."

He told me I still turned him on.

We've been together for about a year but we weren't living together. He was staying at his mom's and I lived with my sisters in the Bronx. I'm sexy as I can ever be, standing 5'1, jet black tress which resembled a horse's mane, very shiny. My hair falls past my ass. That night it was wavy and loose. Ernesto loves when I wear my hair out like that. There I was bent over and driving him crazy.

He came behind me; leaning over and whispered "I'm getting some tonight."

I smiled and said "Oh yeah,"

He responded, "Hell yeah, you are fucking driving me crazy."

I shook my ass to tease him some more. He would have taken me down, right there, had there not been three other crew members in the building with us.

My body is banging, weighing 120 lbs, 34B breasts, 24 inch waist and 38 inch hips. He pulled my head back and pushed his tongue deep into my mouth. *Fuck*, I was just as hungry for him. I missed his dick inside of me. Mind you we still had two more restaurants to clean after this one. His whispered to me that his dick was throbbing but he would hold off till we were done. I tried to estimate how long it would be before we would be done seeing each place took roughly two hours to clean. It felt like time was going extra slow. When we would get in the van to head over to another chain Ernesto would tease me. He brushed his hand against my ass.

Ernesto said "Kayla this is my ass."

I turned around and smiled and said "Maybe." I enjoyed teasing him. He brought the freak out of me; there was no question about it. For him it was whenever, wherever and however. I find him very enticing.

Ernesto stands 5'8, dark tan complexion, slim. He has plenty of tattoos all over his body. It drives me crazy because I love the bad boy look. He has dark eyes and his hair is shaved down low to his head. Ernesto had a goatee and I love the way it feels against me when we kiss.

Finally we were done with work. It was four in the morning when we headed to the train station in Queens. We were in Astoria headed back to the boogie down Bronx. I knew we looked cute as we held hands, walking down the stairs. He was my man and I was his girl and we were in love. We were waiting for the number seven train and at that time of the morning it always proved unpredictable.

Ernesto said "I know I can't wait till we get home. Hell I want you now Kayla."

I smiled at him with a wicked grin.

He looked up and down the platform, no one was in sight. He looked across the platform, there were a few people but not too many. I was standing, looking to see if the train was coming. Ernesto's dick was hard as he watched my ass. He walked over to me and started to kiss the back of my neck. I moaned at the very sensation of his lips because it made me moist.

"Pa you starting…?"

"No," he responded. "I'm finishing what I started earlier."

"Right here," I asked? Ernesto sucked on my neck answering my question. My pussy was in pure heat and with his body so close to mines it made me cum instantly. "Pa," I moaned. "There are people on the other platform."

"So," he responded. "Who cares they ain't watching us. Come on ma give me some." He begged.

He grabbed my ass in his hands and brushed his hard dick against it. *Damn*, his dick was big. I knew there was no way in hell I was gonna resist.

Shit, never had and never will, fuck what you heard.

He pulled my sweats down just below my ass. *Fuck it* I thought as I popped my ass out a little more to give him some leverage. He inserted his rod pumping deep into my pussy. He pulled on my hair pumping faster inside of my wet walls. I peeked over to the other side of the platform and there was a man watching us. I turned my head slightly embarrassed but not caring at the same time. I began to cum down his long shaft. Ernesto moved faster as he saw the train approaching the platform. He started to breath heavy and grunt. He released as the train conductor made eye contact with him. After ejaculating inside of me, we quickly fixed ourselves and got on the train.

We were heading home. We both smiled as we sat in our chairs. I looked out the window. The man who I made eye contact with had a huge smile on his face. He gave me a thumb's up. I laughed and told Ernesto as I put my head on his chest.

He chuckled and said. "I'm the luckiest man there is. My girl is whenever, wherever and however…" His eyes became droopy.

I just smiled and said "Damn right, I'm your personal freak Papi."

Feeling Naughty
Monica Martinez

I was horny this one particular day. I felt like being a naughty girl. I called Andre, a guy I had been dating. I knew I wouldn't be able to see him until the weekend. We were both busy with work, and he lived about an hour from me. His phone rang and rang until I got the voicemail.

I left a message "Hey Chulo, it's me Natalie. Give me a call." I wanted him, and my body was calling for him.

He returned my call within minutes. "Babe what's going on?" he said once I answered.

I asked if he got my message.

"No," he responded. "Just saw your number and called you right away. What's up ma?"

I told him, "Hopefully you."

He giggled.

I told him I didn't want to wait till the weekend to see him. My body was craving and needing him now. I begged him to leave work. He agreed. We would meet somewhere in the middle of both our areas.

We arrived at the same time in the Bronx at the "telly". We got out of our cars, kissed each other hungrily. I reached for his dick which was already hard. I moaned, "I want you."

He smiled and said "Mamita, I want you just as bad".

He was a sexy motherfucker for sure. Andre is 5'8, 140 lbs, nice slim build, caramel complexion and dark brown eyes. He has a nice size dick and his tongue game, well, let's just say, dude should give lessons.

We went inside the hotel to check in. Held hands as we headed to our room. I was wearing a long rain jacket and boots with a nice little surprise for him underneath. He wouldn't know till we got inside the room.

I closed the door once we got in, pushed him onto the

bed. I told him not to move. I knew he would go nuts once he saw what I was wearing. I stand 5'4, 135 lbs, 32D, 23, 38, olive complexion, green eyes and my hair blonde. I stood in front of him as I untied my jacket. He started to go crazy because I had on a little black thong with the matching bra and my black thigh high boots. He couldn't believe I came out of the house like that.

I told him "I was feeling naughty today."

"Shit baby, I could tell" was his response.

He stood, took the belt to my jacket, lifted my hands over my head and told me not to move. He tied my hands together with the belt, while he kissed me. I moaned because I was wet from all the excitement. He turned me to face the wall and kissed the back of my neck and then started sucking on an earlobe.

He worked his way down to my back, getting on his knees and going down to the tip of my thong. He turned me around, now my pussy was in his face. He proceeded to remove my thong with his teeth. I wanted to grab his head and shove it into my wetness, but my hands were tied. I couldn't.

I told him, "Go for it."

Andre started to lick my thighs, took his thumb to play with my clit. My sweet liquid began to cascade down my legs.

He saw it flowing down. It made him moan. He proceeded to take his tongue and stick it back into my pussy. It made the hair on the back of my neck stand. I arched my back so 'kitty' could get closer to his mouth. I moved my hips with the rhythm of his tongue, which was going in circles around my 'gem'. How I love the way he makes me feel. He makes me moist.

"Natalie, you like that?" he asked.

I licked my lips and murmured a "yes..." out. He took his hands and pinched my nipples softly. His lips left my sweetness as he moved to my stomach and licked around my belly ring. He continued to my breasts and removed my bra to suck on my dark circles. He bit them softly, sucking them hard, while his fingers found my clit again. He sucked on me leaving hickeys on my breasts. Milk dripped from my nipples, this excited him. He drank it like a baby would. I moaned wanting to touch him but couldn't. "Baby" I pleaded with him "Please enter me."

Andre kissed me, licked my neck and brushed his lips against mine. I could smell my nectar on his mouth. It smelled delicious. I asked for a kiss. He thrashed his tongue into mine. I kissed him trying to savour the flavour. He began to dry hump me. I felt his dick against my stomach. It was hard, just the way I like it. It was showing me how much he wanted me. I requested for him to give me what I needed. He turned me around with my back facing him. My hands were leaning on the bed still tied. He pulled my butt cheeks apart, entered my canal with such a force. I came instantly on his pipe. My body shivered. He continued to stroke me hard and fast, grabbed my hair and started pulling it with each thrust.

I screamed out "Oh my God" loudly. I enjoyed the rough sex he was providing. I loved to feel his sac smacking against my sweet lips.

He moved with such intensity. I felt his dick growing inside of me with each stroke. He spoke his naughty thoughts to me. I felt him at his peak.

I begged for it. "Baby, give it to me." Just as he was about to cum he took his dick out of me and turned me around, pushed me down to my knees. I wanted his rod in my mouth. I wanted to feel his hot juice squirt down my throat. I looked at him as he was about to thrust into my mouth, gave him a wicked one.

I said to him in Spanish "Dame me papi por favour…" Speaking Spanish drove him insane. He came instantly in my mouth. His body quivered as he grunted. I contracted on his dick pulling it deeper into my mouth making sure his cum filled my mouth.

He lifted me back to my feet, untied me and laid me on the bed. He reached his arms out for me and told me to sit on his dick. I started to ride his thick rod.

Damn he felt good.

I wanted to bring myself to pleasure again. I rode faster, deeper strokes as I played with my nipples for him. I felt my nectar starting to drip onto his shaft. I moaned screaming to him "Glad I didn't wait to get some of this good loving." I went as deep as I could on his rod and hit my g-spot sending myself into pure bliss. I called out his name and screamed "Diablo." There were tears running down my eyes as the orgasm hit with such force.

I wanted this type of loving all the time, shit I wanted him to be my man forever.

We had only booked the room for three hours and we approached it very fast. The phone rang. It was our time to get moving. We showered. I put back on what little apparel I had.

He looked at me and said "Damn babe, I really can't believe you stepped out like that?"

He was getting hard again. He said it was so sexy for me to step out wearing very little clothing. He loved the fact that I was daring.

I told him not to return to work that we should go to my place and take this through the night. He followed me home.

In my car I thought *being naughty can be a good thing.*

Two Ships Passing

Monica Martinez

I came home late one night. My man was sleeping when I walked into the bedroom. For the last couple of day we had been two ships passing each other. It was the holiday season and I took up a second job. I was working late nights and he during the day. I had been longing for him, wanting to make love him. I began to get undressed from the long stressful day and looked at him as he lay on our bed so peacefully. It made me hot. We hadn't made love in almost four days. When you go from making love every day to not getting it all, well, let's just say it's not cool at all.

I closed my eyes briefly and envisioned we were making

passionate love. Not wanting to disturb him but at the same time wanting to have some pleasure, I debated whether or not to wake him. As I got closer to the bed he moved slightly turning around.

He groggily said, "Hello."

Instantly my mouth went down onto his dick. The very thought he was awake had me crazy. I wanted him bad.

I played with his dick through his boxers at first, pulling at it softly with my teeth. He moaned. That gave me an indication, he wanted me to proceed. I took his long rod out of the boxers and sucked on him until his shaft was covered in salvia. I licked the tip of his now hardened stick. I placed my lips over head of his dick.

I sucked on just the tip and stroked his shaft. I began moving my head in circular motions, and then devoured all of his manhood deep into my mouth. Steve tasted good and felt good. The heat from him was evident enough to know he was also in need of me.

He called out my name, "Zahira," it made me very aggressive.

I pulled his boxers off with a lot of force. I took a step back, stood before him in my panties admiring his hardness. I just wanted to sit on it. It was standing at attention and calling out to me. I couldn't take it anymore. I took my panties off and jumped into the bed.

I stood above him for a moment, gave him a devilishly nasty grin. Then I positioned myself in squat and sat on Steve's erection. I started moving on him like I was trying to win a championship for bronco riding. He began moaning with pleasure, loving the aggression I was showing.

"Baby... what's gotten... into you...?" he asked moaning and beginning to pant.

I had no response and continued riding his rod playing with my clit all the while. I immediately brought myself to pleasure. Nectar dripped down onto his sac.

The smell of sex filled our room, *damn how I miss the smell of us* I thought. It was bringing me to a high that I sure as hell didn't want to come down from. I continued riding him, digging my nails into his chest, and biting him.

He lifted me off of him with abruptness and started to kiss on my neck. Steve moved his head down to my nipples. He sucked on them sending chills down my spine.

I screamed out his name begging him for more...

He entered my tight hole with such force, grabbing my ass pushing me up and down onto his dick. This excited me so much I arched my back cumming once again. I felt my flow release like a waterfall onto him.

He screamed "Baby, ride this dick, take your dick."

I continued going fast, grinding, hitting my G-spot since I had full control. Just as I was about to orgasm again, he brought his hands to my neck choking me slightly.

Fuck. I came to a full orgasm. I started screaming like a wild ass bitch. "Oh… my… God." My body twitched and jerked.

Steve couldn't take it anymore. He switched positions, and he laid me down onto our bed. He began to kiss my neck as he played with my hardened clit. He knew how to make me feel good.

I was still on my screaming tip. "Don't stop this amazing love session."

He took his hard dick, inserted it back into my wet walls.

"Papi, it feels so… good." I murmured submissively subdued.

He gave me deep long strokes. I wrapped my legs around his back. I grabbed his ass and pushed him deeper into my pussy. I couldn't help but scratched his back and suck on his neck.

"I love your dick, the hardness of it. How it fills me up."

He loves when I speak to him like that.

Steve moved faster and deeper, I felt his nature growing bigger inside my wetness. I screamed how much I loved him, thrashing my tongue into his mouth. I was losing control again and felt another orgasm coming. He yelled out how much he loved me, how tight my pussy felt. I knew he would explode at any moment. I had to share the moment with him by cumming with him. I moved closer on him to get him deeper inside of her.

"Baby...." I screamed as my body began to shiver. I scratched deep into his back. He grabbed my ass, definitely leaving his hand prints. "Yes Papi, this pussy belongs to you. Give me my dick...." I yelled.

He started to grunt and then he exploded. We had come together, both breathing heavy, our hearts beating fast.

"Damn, bad girl, that was so good."

I was out of breath but managed to whisper this, "Baby, our love is amazing. I missed you so much."

I silently thought *when will our lives get back on track, when we are not two ships passing one another?*

Jacuzzi

Monica Martinez

$\mathcal{I}$ needed to relax after a long day of work. As soon as I got home I started a hot bubble bath. They usually calm me down. I hoped it would be the case today. Work had been stressful for the last couple of days, not to mention my cycle just ended. I'm feeling horny. *It has been a minute* I thought to myself. I undressed and stepped into the hot, steamy water and rested my head against the bath pillow. I closed my eyes and attempted to meditate. My jump off Julio came to mind.

I met him about a month ago on my way to work. Being newly divorced I knew I didn't want a relationship, just wanted sex. Julio fit the description for the time being.

Julio 5'9, 165 lbs, fit, with seductive hazel eyes, black wavy hair and cream colored skin. He was well equipped. He definitely knew how to work it and his eating game was tight. It had only been a few days since I last saw him. The thought of him put a smile on my face like always.

I lathered the soap and cleaned around my breast. I began to get excited when I touched them, playing with my nipples one by one while I thought about the last time I was with Julio. The way my 'tulip' was in his mouth, as he ate me. I lost myself in thought caressing my breast thinking about how he sucked on them. Julio always had me moaning. I thought about his foreplay because it was definitely hot and on point. I remembered a time when I arrived at his house; he immediately began to kiss and undress me the moment I stepped in. He continued to tease me as we headed to his bedroom.

I clearly pictured the way he had me against his dresser, ass up and face down. That's my favorite position. It drives me nuts. He pushed his tongue so deep into my pussy, I creamed all over his mouth. My pussy began to pulsate in the tub while I reminisced. I continued to lather my body and became even hornier. My fingers were at the entrance of my tunnel. I started fingering myself I was turned on so much. I started to grind my hips deeper onto my fingers, imagining I was riding Julio's cock. This excited me more. I wanted to bring pleasure to myself. I decided to turn on the jets, lifting my legs so the jet could hit directly on my clit. The flow from the jet was strong; it felt good on my 'gem'. I moved up and down against the rapid stream.

I thought about how good it felt to have Julio's hard stick inside of me. The jets had so much force it wouldn't be long before I would cum. The warm water hitting my clit with such a powerful force, it made me scream Julio's name. My body jerked back and forth, I was panting. My heart was beating so fast. I came hard. After releasing with such intensity, there was nothing I could do except lay in the tub. After ten minutes of my 'pearl' throbbing, I got out and dried myself.

I decided reminiscing should always lead to having the real thing again. I grabbed my phone, tapped out Julio's number and left him a message…

"Hey Julio, this is Adrianna I'm in need."

That was all I had to say. In a few he would be at my doorsteps and ready for action. *This jump-off stuff was good shit. Not being married was even better* I thought to myself as I luxuriated across my bed waiting for him to come over.

Chance Encounter
Monica Martinez

We women know within the first five minutes of meeting a single man whether or not we will sleep with him. Make no mistake about it; he doesn't pick us we pick him. However, a man who acquires my attention is far and few in between. A rare occasion, however, when it happens, you better step aside and move out my way so long as he is not attached to someone else. I sure as hell with not play second to anyone, I'm far too beautiful and think too highly of myself to be put in such a situation. I will do what I need to do to make him mines. Bear in mind, my qualities, yes the check off list. You ladies know exactly what I'm talking about...

A man has to be tall, dark and handsome. Yes, I said it. I admit to being vain, however, my requirements don't stop there. He must also be intelligent and able to host a good conversation. I love to talk. He better be up to date on current news, politics, history, science and even food. He has to be a take charge type of man. Lord knows he also needs to have major skills in the bedroom; otherwise he gets tossed aside. If he can't give me better satisfaction than my Pearl Butterfly Vibrator, he is not needed. I am nobody's mother and I am sure as hell not going to teach a grown man what is necessary for the bedroom. Forget that. Grant it he will definitely have to get accustomed to my body, but as you already know first impressions are everything, especially in the bedroom because that is going to determine whether or not I will be coming back.

Trust me I stay on top of my sex game as well as taking good care of myself. I don't believe in letting myself go. As vain as I am I refuse too. I can put some twenty year olds to shame. No offense youngins' you girls really need to step up to the plate. I know how to keep a man coming back for more, you best believe. I still have the ex's begging to come back or wanting more of me. I don't go there simply because you are an ex for a reason. I may have slipped in the past because I was extremely horny, however since the Pearl Butterfly has come into my life I don't have to anymore.

Don't get it twisted either I'm not addicted to my toys. I definitely enjoy the real thing. However, I will use it when I'm not with someone simply because I am choosey as to who will share my bed or my life…

I was scheduled to work the Circle of Sister Expo in NYC. I saw him out the corner of my eye. *God Damn* he was everything I could ask for on the outside. Nice Chocolate brother standing 6'2 looked to be about 175 lbs. His body was sick, meaning good. I licked my lips as he past my booth. I watched to see where he was heading. Turned out he was one of the models for a calendar, which was directly across from my area. Nonetheless, I was thrilled. His full lips were inviting, he had a broad nose and high cheek bones. He had a goat-tee. *Damn* he was the definition of handsome, fine, good-looking, whatever word you want to use for it.

He looked my way and nodded a gesture of hello and his dark brown eyes caressed my body. I was hot and for a moment I thought someone turned up the heat. He smiled, showcasing his beautiful white teeth. I thought now *if he has brains behind the smile and he was single it would be perfect.* While I know the perfect man doesn't exist although we are raised to believe in this knight and shining armor he was close. I glanced at his big hands and there was no sign of a ring *so far so good* I thought. His feet were big as well. Immediately I went into lust mode *mmmmm, mmmmm, mmmmm...* Yes we ladies have also been taught big hands and big feet equal big man down below.

Shoot. I was ready to find out. I knew if dude wasn't married, engaged or had a girlfriend I was going to give him whatever his heart desired, provided he met my requirements of being intelligent. It would be a shame if he wasn't, an automatic turn off for me. I crossed my fingers and tried to concentrate on working the booth and getting as many sales as I could for the day.

I kept on praying *let him come over*. It seemed the stars were aligned in my favor. He made his way over to my booth, formally introduced himself.

"Hello my name is Troy. I had to come over here to meet you."

I smiled and put my hand out for a handshake.

I introduced myself, "Hi Troy, pleasure to meet you. I'm Maritza."

"I had to come over here simply because you are something else. Your energy is driving me insane."

I smiled. His game was a little weak but just because he was so damn cute I played along.

"Troy may I ask a question?"

He shook his head yes "Are you married, have a girlfriend?"

He smiled and gladly responded "No I'm not married. I don't have a girlfriend, hell I don't even have kids."

Excellent were my thoughts. We agreed to meet after the Expo was over for drinks. I was dead ass tired. It had been a long day. Troy came over to the booth at exactly ten o'clock to help me pack my things away. It was a sweet gesture. I gladly accepted help. I sent my girls home for the evening and we agreed we meet back at eight the next morning.

Troy asked me if I was married, engaged, or had a boyfriend.

I chuckled and responded, "Nope. I'm single for the moment."

He said "Wow, guess I just got lucky."

We both laughed.

An hour later we were done packing all of my supplies. Troy helped me to my truck. I asked where he was staying for the evening. I was booked at the Bentley Hotel down on 62nd street. He responded I'm actually staying at a friend's place in Harlem.

I invited him to my hotel because I knew there was a lounge on the 22nd floor and it would be a great place to talk and get to know each other.

We arrived at the hotel within ten minutes. I parked the car and off we went to the lounge. It was empty; *perfect* I thought. We ordered some food. Troy doesn't drink, smoke, eat pork, or even red meat. I was impressed. He was an intelligent dude and he had my attention. *Too good to be true let's see what else is going on with him?* Troy lived in Philly and I lived in Brentwood. Not sure how it was going to work but it was definitely worth a try. Troy also proved to have a very busy scheduled with his upcoming modeling career. It was fine with me as I am just as busy. He was seven years younger then me. I wasn't quite sure what I could do with him.

It was two in the morning when I looked down at my watch. I knew I would only have a few hours to sleep. It was time to end our date. I had to admit I was enjoying Troy.

I smiled and said, "We need to end our date. I need to be at the expo bright and early tomorrow."

I could tell he wasn't ready to leave he was enjoying me as much as I was him. He reluctantly stood.

"Maritza I love our conversation. It's too bad we need to end our night." He made sure to get me to my room safely. He was going to take a cab into Harlem. I felt safe with him. I don't know what came over me but I invited him to stay the night with me.

He didn't decline the offer. However, I made it very clear to him we would not be sexing or doing anything close to it. He agreed he would be the perfect gentleman. True to his word we cuddled the entire night. I felt safe with him. Still, in my mind the thoughts came *too good to be true*.

We awoke and took turns showering and rushed out to the Javits. We both worked with smiles on our faces for the entire day. He joined me for lunch and we spoke about how comfortable we were with one another. I was happy he was single everything would work to out perfectly. At the end of the day, Troy once again helped pack everything and aided me in loading my truck. He was headed to Philly and I was headed to Long Island. We kissed goodbye and promised to stay in touch. His kiss sent me into heavenly bliss.

Troy called me everyday for the next two weeks. We

made plans for me to go to Philly and hang out with him for the weekend. I drove three hours to him. He was a perfect gentleman for the entire weekend. He took me out to dinner, slept on his couch while giving his bedroom to me. We went to the mall, he catered to me and it was very sweet. I was enjoying the attention he was providing. He didn't make a move on me and it was perfect. Although I knew he would be getting the goods regardless, he was playing his position correctly.

We continued for a month with me going to Philly one weekend and him coming to New York the next. Troy never stepped out of line. I loved it. Going on our second month it was time for Troy to get the prize. I had it all planned out carefully. I had cooked for him. My bedroom was set to perfection.

Troy arrived at nine that day. He entered the house to a candle lit dinner. He smiled and asked, "What's the occasion?"

I smiled and responded, "The occasion is us."

He smiled and asked to skip dinner. I was happy he did. I wanted to make love to him. He lifted me off my feet and kissed me with hunger. He carried me to my bedroom.

Upon opening the door he smiled. "Maritza you went all out. I'm supposed to be doing this for you."

He gently kissed me while lifting my dress over my head. He was surprised to see the little black garter belt with the thigh high stockings and black bra. "Wow" was all he could say.

He laid me on the bed as we kissed. He moved to kiss my neck down to my breast. He took my nipples in his mouth, one by one, sucked softly and lightly bit on them. I moaned as his touch was out of this world. Taking his tongue down my belly and circling my belly button, I was losing control. My pussy was throbbing and beyond being saturated. He moved to my pussy kissed her softly and moved to my inner thighs, biting them softly. He did this a few more times giving me a lick here and there on my slits. Jeez he was bringing me pure pleasures with every move. Troy spread my swollen lips apart and sucked on my clit making my stomach contract as the orgasm hit. I screamed while he continued sucking and licking. He inserted a finger inside my pussy while eating me out.

I was crazed. I begged for more.

"Troy give me more. Please, give me more…"

Troy moved his tongue deeper into my pussy, as his finger hit my g-spot. I released my juices onto his tongue. He drank and moaned at the same time. Troy moved away from my sweetness and kissed me softly on my lips.

As I inhaled my essence from his mouth it drove me wild.

It was my turn to please him.

I reached for his manhood and started to stroke. As I stroked it I was amazed. Troy was well endowed *God Damn I'm bout to have so much fun.*

I kissed Troy on his lips and worked my way down to his huge cock. I placed the tip in my mouth slowly. I had to mentally prepare myself to relax my throat as I was going to deep throat his dick no matter how big it was. I pulled in the tip to mid point and looked to see his reaction. He was impressed, I could tell. I worked his cock like a porn star that enjoyed her job immensely.

Troy held onto the back of my neck as he pushed his cock deep down my throat. He was moaning. I felt his dick contract as he was getting ready to release his cum. I pulled it out and stroked him till he gave me a complete facial. He went nuts moaning. I ended it by smacking his dick onto my tongue.

He lifted me to the bed and turned me doggy style. He went down south once again. He made me cum twice before he entered me. He grabbed my hair and pulled my head back to thrust his tongue in my mouth as his dick went deep inside me. I gasped for air, God damn his dick was huge. He moved inside of me as if he were made for me. The fit was prefect. He pushed deep inside of me. His dick was good. I screamed out his name over and over again. Troy continued to push back and forth into my pussy.

He wrapped my hair around his arm and pulled my head back asking me if I like what he was doing. Troy smacked my ass and grabbed both cheeks with his big hands. Holding me tight and pressing deeper into me, I screamed with pleasure.

He pulled out of me and turned me around to face him. He sucked on my breast as he entered inside of me. He moved slowly and passionately inside of my walls making me have another orgasm.

"Maritza" he yelled looking in my face. "I'm going to cum."

I wrapped my legs around his back and arched myself to get closer to him. I felt his body tremble as he shot his cum deep inside of me. Troy continued to push inside of me till his manhood went soft.

We cuddled for the remainder of our evening. I'm so glad I took a chance on our encounter. He is a wonderful man and we are scheduled to marry this July. His modeling career is flourishing. I am proud of my man.

Silent Caller

Monica Martinez

It's was about midnight the first time I received his call. Hello I answer into my phone. No response, hello I said again, still no answer. Immediately I hung up and not even five seconds later it's ringing again. I picked up not saying anything; he doesn't say a thing but I can hear him breathing on the phone. I hung up and turned my cell off. This went on for the entire week at the same time of the evening. I started to become frustrated but what can I do if he won't tell me who he is or what he wants. I don't have a clue as to who it might be. I rack my brain over and over. I think about the guys I've dated and possible broke up with because they didn't meet m   uirements.

One month has gone by. He was religious in his calling. I started yelling into the phone. This is aggravating not to mention annoying. Finally he said something, but shit I can't recognize the voice. He was disguising it.

He said to me, "I poured out my heart to you. Why did you do me like that?"

I said "Excuse me? Who the hell is this?"

He said nothing. I put my phone on mute and he stayed on the phone breathing for at least twenty minutes. It's been three months and he was faithful to his calling ritual. Once I screamed into the phone, "This is super annoying." and began chewing gum in his ear. I placed the phone down once again on mute because I know his pattern. If I hang up he would only call me back. So I left him hanging on mute.

I called my cell phone carrier which is Nextel, they tell me I can block private numbers, but shit, most of my friends and sometimes even clients called private. I headed down to the precinct to see if they could do anything. They told me to change my number. I really couldn't do it because I've had the same number for over ten years. I'll deal with him my way, I think to myself as I left the police station.

One Saturday night I was sleeping and my phone vibrated. I answered saying hello in a whisper. He didn't say anything. I knew better than to hang up on him; I just placed the phone back on my nightstand and tried to sleep. However, I heard him breathing heavy into the phone as if he were doing something weird. I lifted my head and stared at my phone thinking maybe I was hearing things.

I grabbed it and put it to my ear. He was moaning. I listened and it sounded as if he was jerking off. I could hear his hands beating his dick, oh my goodness. I quickly severed the connection on him. He rang my phone at least fourteen times and each time I ignored his calls. I finally shut the phone off.

He stopped for about two weeks and it was great. I figured he was finally done with harassing me. I was wrong. He doesn't let more than a month go by before he is calling me again. So now it's me, him and the mute button. He has my interest because I'd like to know who I left such an impression on, for he has been calling me for over a year now.

Tonight will be no different as my phone rings. I think it's my client because she and I were working hard to meet a deadline.

"Hello" I answer. No response, so I know it's my silent caller at this moment. I do my ritual by putting him on mute and continue to go about my business. I realize I have to hang up on him in order to keep the phone clear for my client. I hang up and call my client to inform her of the situation. My phone beeps again. It's him.

I answer, "Hello?" still nothing. I finally ask "What do you want?" still nothing. I ask, "Do I know you?"

He answers me "Not as well as I'd like."

I ask again, "What do you want?"

He responds, "I want you to lie on your back."

So he wants to play, I think to myself.

I'm single what the hell?

I lay on my back with a smirk on my face. I ask him "Why?"

He tells me he wants me to relax as he takes me on a journey. He asks me to close my eyes; I do so. He inquires about what I am wearing. I tell him I have on my black silk nightgown. He wants details, I explain to him it's black and it goes down to my ankles. It has lace around my breast area. He asks if I have any panties on. I think to myself

I'm crazy because this will only heighten his calls to me more often than not. I hesitated and whispered no. He says perfect are your eyes closed? I responded yes they are. Take your right hand and caress your breast for me, he instructs. Please make your nipples erect he adds. Automatically my hand started to do as he commanded. I moved my right hand over my breasts awaking my nipples.

My dark berries were fully elevated as I let out a sexy little purr into the phone. He told me his man hood is fully erect and in his hand. He said he will stroke to the rhythm of my breathing. I'm wet at the moment, the unknown has me excited and captivated.

He called my name, "Janice…"

I opened my eyes wide in wonderment. He really knows who I am.

He tells me its okay and said, close your eyes again. I close them. My pussy throbbed with thoughts of my silent caller. I'm curious as to what he looks like, how tall he is.

He breathes into the phone and whispers, "Janice, I want to suck the honey out of you till you scream, fuck me out of the top of your lungs."

My heart beat starts to raise as my hand traces the outline of my 'pussy'. I lift my nightgown up and start to rub on my clit as he made a slurping sound as if he were really eating me out.

"Janice," he called out. "I am down on you, spreading your wings apart." Damn, I think to myself, he may just really know me cuz I call my girl below my butterfly. He mentioned wings...? Oh well fuck it, I'm here and enjoying it.

I rubbed my clit harder and faster as my liquid cascaded from my lips. I moaned into the phone, "Oh yeah, just like that."

His breathing became heavier I can hear that he is about to erupt.

Oh snap. My other line rings. It's a private call, which means it's my client. I ask for him to please hold. I clicked over a little flustered as she just stopped me from probably making the biggest mistake ever...

Private Show
Monica Martinez

$\mathcal{J}$ahira worked a peep show booth on the weekends. She needed the extra money to support her three year old son. Her son's father was in jail for the last two years. She didn't think it was a horrible job simply because it was quite harmless in her eyes. The men didn't get to touch her. They only got to watch her through a glass window.

She went to work one night and started to get ready. She put on her little maid outfit with the garter belt. She grabbed her red high heels, put on her make-up and a wig with long red hair. She figured she'd rather be safe than sorry not wanting someone to recognize her, although she made sure she worked in a whole different town. Her bell rang, which meant she had a customer. She had to be ready at any given time...

The curtain opened. She turned her music on with her back facing the man watching her. She began moving her body side to side, swaying her hips. Her ass was jiggling to the beat of a dance song called *whine up on me*. She made her booty clap against the pole in the center of her stage.

Nelson was the man on the other side of the window. He was seated so one couldn't tell how tall he is. He stood 6'5, weighed about 250 lbs; his skin color a shade of cream. He was a basketball player for one of the major leagues. He kept his sunglasses on trying to make sure no one recognized him. He was very lanky, his fingers were very long. He wore a size twenty shoe. His face displayed a straight nose, a goatee and his was hair in a short afro. He would frequent peep shows to masturbate. It was the sort of shit he liked to do.

It became a habit of his while on the road because he had recently gotten sued by a woman he had sex with. She sued him for ripping her uterus with his fifteen inch cock. Most women were scared when they came across him, only allowing him to put the tip in. It was thick as well, so it would break the lining of the women's pussy, sending them to their doctor to sew it back together. He understood he was cursed. It was best if he just masturbated to women behind glass. He wouldn't be able to hurt them that way. He watched Jahira move her ass back and forth.

Jahira's body was tight. She was 5'9, weighed 160 lbs, thick in all the right places. Her hips and ass measured at 44 inches, her waist tiny at 25 inches and she had a firm 32D cup. Jahira turned around to face her new customer to make sure he got his money's worth. He paid a thousand dollars for a half hour show. Jahira liked what she saw when she turned around. It was easier to do shows for good looking men as opposed to dirty old fat men. She danced to the music, touching herself with her clothing still on. She moved herself up and down the pole doing stunts for her new client. She slid down the pole rubbing her pussy on it. Nelson's dick was erect. He unzipped his pants to pull out his long rod. He took it out, the full length of it springing into existence. He took a small bottle of lubrication from a pocket, squeezing some onto his hand. He started to stroke his dick.

Jahira was shocked and amazed at the length of his cock. She had never seen anything like it before. Most men who came in for a peep show had tiny dicks. She tried not to drool at it as he made it shiny with his lube. His dick was long and thick resembled a dildo she had. She became wet and her pussy twitched. She slowly took off her dress then stood in the middle of the room, before him and his dick. She was left only with bra, garter belt and her thigh high lace black stockings.

She played with her breasts, rubbing them with her bra still on. Jahira bounced her breasts for Nelson, grabbing at them throwing her head back. She reached to her back to release her breasts from the bra. Her breasts presented themselves. Nelson was pleased that her tits were big and firm. She played with her nipples pinching them, sucking on her fingers and making circles around her nipples with the saliva. Nelson continued to stroke his dick slowly enjoying the view of the very sexy woman on the other side of the glass.

Jahira wanted to get a closer look at his big cock. She only thought dildos were made that size. She crawled over to the glass to get a better view. She pushed her breasts to the window and Nelson's hand went to reach as if he could feel her. Jahira grinded against the glass and began to rub her pussy with her fingers. She was dripping as placed two fingers inside of her moist pussy then she brought them in and out. She took her soaked fingers and wiped them on the glass. Nelson started to stroke his dick harder and faster. She was making him very excited. He never experienced a dancer like this. It was almost as if she enjoyed the fact his cock was so big and thick.

Jahira licked her lips, brought her fingers to her mouth sucked on them. She loved the way she tasted. She was sweet. She went down on the floor, lifted her legs, bringing her pussy as close to the window as possible. She opened her legs wide. Nelson was going crazy watching her pussy almost press against the window.

Her pussy finally connected with glass. She moved up and down the glass leaving a glaze of pussy juice on it. She was turned on watching him stand and stroke what seemed to be at least fourteen to fifteen inches. She couldn't believe the length and girth of it. She wanted an even closer look. It looked fucking tasty. She hadn't had a good fuck in years. She moved her pussy in circular motions while reaching for one of the numerous toys on the floor. She grabbed a dildo. Nelson was on the verge of cumming. She moved the black dildo in and out of her fat pussy. Her dildo seemed to be just as big as his cock. It was a dildo with a suction cup. Jahira rose off the floor and stuck the dildo to the glass window. She straddled it looking him dead in his eyes from behind. Nelson couldn't hold his cum and shot his load onto the window. Jahira looked at the amount of semen he shot. Her eyes widened. She was amazed and aroused.

His cum was thick and white. She wondered how it would have felt to have him cum on her breasts. She moved harder onto the dildo with her hands on the window. She moved deeper onto her fourteen inch dildo taking it completely inside of her wet pussy. Nelson was pleased. Noticeably, she was enjoying it. The buzzer went off, which meant the show was over. Jahira didn't want the show to end. She wanted to come out of her window, go straight into the room and fuck him. However, she knew it was against policy. He was just another customer. She was about to clean herself. There would be time before another customer. Then bell went off and the curtains opened again…

Nelson was standing, watching her. He deposited more money, and did so fast…

Jahira swore with delight. She didn't even have time to take the dildo off the glass. She continued where she left off and started fucking the dildo again. She was still open and wet. She did that for a short while, then slid herself off the dildo and showed her ass and excavated pussy to him. She took the dildo off the glass stuck it on the floor, straddled it and bounced on it. Nelson was still standing, with his erect dick. He watched her insert the fake cock completely inside of her.

Damn, what did he have to do to get her outside of this window? He was thinking as he stroked. He looked for a piece of paper to write down a question for her. He found one on the floor. He wrote, 'I would love to see you outside of here if that's possible'? He took off his sunglasses so she could see the sincerity in his eyes. He possessed the sexiest black eyes she had ever seen. Fuck she wanted so bad to go against the policy. Not to mention there were camera's watching to make sure she didn't do anything she wasn't supposed to. She shook her head, no, looked at the mirrors showing him they were being watched. He realized what she was pointing out to him without really showing him. He sat down and let her finish her show. Nelson watched her during her shift which was four hours. He dropped eight thousand dollars on her, so no one would see her for the rest of the night. After she cleaned the window and the rest of her area she headed back to her dressing room. She was more than pleased with the money she made tonight.

She got dressed in jeans, took off her wig letting her

black hair loose and threw on an Ed Hardy sweater. She grabbed sneakers and headed out of the club. The customer with the monstrous dick was obviously rich. She got to leave with sixty percent of the money. It would be more than enough to hold her over for the next two month.

When she exited she noticed a Hummer limousine waiting at the side of the club. Nelson rolled his window down and asked her if she would join him for drinks. Jahira smiled because she was hoping he would wait for her. Technically she wasn't on company's time anymore. In spite of that, she made sure none of the bouncers or any of the other working girls were looking before she snuck inside the limo.

Once inside the limo he introduced himself to her.

"Nelson…"

"My name is Jahira" she responded.

"You look better with the black hair" He told her.

She laughed, "Well I don't want people to really know what I look like." "Is this the only job you have?" He asked.

"I need to do this on a part-time basis," She giggled. "My son's father is a dead beat, currently in jail. I need the money to support my lil man."

They drove around the city for a few hours getting to know one another. During the limo driving, Nelson said,

"I'm a basket ball player"

Jahira thought what the fuck do you need to come to the peep show dude could have any chick he wanted. She didn't believe him. It was crazy.

She asked. "Are you serious?"

"Of course I am. Why would I lie to you?"

"Wow," she responded "Are you married?"

"No, I'm not. The women I've come in contact with are scared of me. They say I'm cursed because of my big dick."

Jahira licked her lips, leaned over to him and she whispered in an ear. "I'm not scared of it. Not one bit..."

Sin City

Monica Martinez

You know the saying: "What happens in Vegas stays in Vegas." That is exactly where I was headed and that is exactly what was going to happen. We both knew. He just didn't know how heavy I was going to put it on him.

I figured I'd take a cab to the airport to meet Alexandro. *Time to be naughty,* I thought as I dressed in my bathroom. Didn't know how I was going to dazzle Alexandro till after I showered, oiled and scented my body. Afterwards it struck me. I decided to adorn a black mini dress which would showcase every womanly curve I own. It would also provide easy access to my goodies. All I could do is giggle. Underneath I would have on a black push up bra and lace thong from Victoria's Secret. The dress along with my Charles David black snakeskin sling backs, which accented my calves were sure to wow him at first sight. I started getting dressed.

The thought of his luscious lips on my sweetness had me wet and quivering. Imagining the softness of his lips touching my 'girl', then having his tongue dash across my 'pearl' and slithering deep into my 'tunnel' was driving me crazy.

I can't wait to feel Alexandro's hands touch me, I'm so anxious to please him in all ways.

Thinking about going to '*Sin City*' made me want to be a bad girl. I was back and forth from the big mirror in my bedroom to the bathroom mirror above the sink. After I was certain I was as adorably sexy as I could be, I grabbed my bag from the living room. It was packed with playful gadgets and clothes. Didn't know which way was which for me I was so excited. I rushed back to the bedroom and glanced pleasingly in the mirror a final time before I headed out the door. I planned to put it on Alexandro the entire weekend.

Damn, I wasn't sure if I was going to let him come up for air. I wanted our intermingling scents to fill each other's nostrils the entire time we were in Vegas. In the cab, on the way to the airport, I had to keep my legs crossed. The driver was looking at me from the rear view mirror while I continued to shift from left to right. My sweetness was throbbing with each second getting closer to Alexandro. I began to shake my legs, like I normally do when I'm nervous, hoping to ease the tension on my 'girl' below. I had to close my eyes trying to stop my stomach from doing butterfly flops inside. I was nervous yet excited, it was the first time we were going on a trip together; the first weekend where it would be just the two of us. *Damn, I should have smoked a joint to ease my nervousness.*

I finally arrived at the airport and stepped out of the cab and headed over to departures, looking for his sexy ass. My phone rang; it was him saying "Boo, I'm on my way to the airport."

"Okay," I responded then decided to go to the bar area. For the first time in my life I thought, *'I need a drink'.* Soon

I was standing at the bar.

The bartender came over and said "Can I help you?" Of course, I had no idea what to order because I don't drink but at the same time I didn't want to look silly. I quickly remembered a drink my girls drank and requested an apple martini. A few minutes later I was sitting at the bar and the drink was in front of me. I paid for it debating whether or not to really drink it. *'Fuck it,'* I thought.

"What's a few sips going to do to me anyway?" I murmured to myself. Two sips later and, *shit*, I was feeling good, bold actually. Our flight was scheduled to depart in two hours, my phone went off again. Alexandro was asking where I was. "I'm over by the bar," I responded.

"Okay Isabella, I'm heading right over."

The airport was busy that day; the bar had a good deal of people within. I saw him the moment he entered the room, *'Diablo'*, I thought to myself. Alexandro hadn't spotted me as of yet. He looked good with his black slacks and gray button down shirt...

...He was wearing black shoes and had a leather bag in his hand. His hair was freshly cut and down to a Caesar. I love that look on him. It made him look fucking incredibly hot. He had just shaved too...

Great because his lips were going to be doing some damage to me.

Waving my arms, I stood so he could spot me. My belly started to flutter...

Here come those dam butterflies; let me sip on this drink again.

As he got closer my stomach simmered down. By now I was comfortable with him. We had been seeing each other for seven months, and there was no need to be nervous or scared. He had this way of making me feel at ease with just a look from his soft brown eyes. The drink was definitely having some type of effect on me.

Alexandro kissed me softly on the lips and took a step back to admire me; the smile on his face said it all. He was satisfied with the outfit I had chosen for him.

Thank goodness...

I needed everything to be *perfect*. I smiled, and leaned into him. With nerve I thrust my tongue into his mouth. I wanted him to know that this weekend we would become one. I needed my passion to show in the kiss I had given to him. He reached for my waist and pulled me even closer to him. Our bodies were connected. My panties were soaked, at that very moment. I let out a little moan during our kiss.

I pulled away and gave him the seductive look I knew he loved. Alexandro once told me my eyes were so sexy when I'm in lust mode. He said my eyes could seduce any man if I chose to.

All he could get out of his mouth was, "Damn Isabella, this is gonna be a wonderful trip."

I whispered in his ear, "Oh, Alexandro you have no idea." He placed his bag down by my barstool and waved the bartender over for a beer. Alexandro went to get the bartenders attention more directly. As I watched him walk the expanse of the bar, I was throbbing beyond control.

He had his Corona in hand heading back towards me. Our eyes locked on one another. He was blocking others from my view. I decided to tease him and show him how much I wanted him. I uncrossed my legs slowly so he could get a glimpse of my lace panties. I teased him more by licking my lips while reaching for my drink. Alexandro licked his juicy-ass lips adjusting his nature in his pants. *Looked like I was waking up that bad boy,* and damn, I was glad because I couldn't wait to feel him inside of me.

He sat in front of me placing his strong hands on my legs. Sweat from the Corona bottle dripped down and fell in between my legs down towards my sweetness. I gave him a look that said *are you going to wipe it?* He reached towards my inner thigh to wipe the trickle of water and brushed his hand against my juicy world. I thought for a moment I was gonna lose my mind because it felt so good. He let out a sigh. I saw Alexandro's dick getting hard through his slacks.

I moaned and said "Mmmmm, Daddy I like the way that felt." He leaned over to give me another kiss as his hand started to explore more of my underworld. He stopped because people were around, he didn't want anyone to see what was about to become all his. I suggested we head back over to the chairs where we could wait for the plane to board. He agreed because he needed to cool down and, Lord knows, I needed to calm myself down. The little I had of my drink had me trippin'. I was ready to take Alexandro right then and there. *Easy...*I told myself... *be easy.* We talked a bit before boarding the plane; we each had carry-on luggage.

Alexandro grabbed both of our bags. As I walked in front of him, I put a little extra *umph* into my stride. Making my hips sway side to side just a little harder, I turned my head over my shoulders to check him out. Just as I wanted,

Alexandro was in a daze mesmerized by my backside.

"Daddy" I called to him and said "you are *sooooooo* gonna get it."

"No, Boo, you're gonna get it," Alexandro responded.

I playfully teased him and questioned, "You promise?"

We boarded the plane and got to our seats. I watched him put the bags overhead. My eyes were staring at the bulk in his pants wondering how big he was, wondering how thick he was. Wondering what he would taste like. Wondering about when he would shoot a lot of cum and whether or not it would taste salty.

I reached for his belt buckle as he was putting the second bag up; he stopped what he was doing to look at me for a second. I just smiled and asked if he needed any help? He chuckled because he knew the kind of help I was implying.

"Yes, Boo, I need help but not here." He said "When we land I'll need lots of help."

I teased him some more and told him, "I'll be more than happy to provide any type of CPR to you."

The plane was small and we were seated at a window that only had two seats. I thought to myself, *perfect* with a wicked grin on my face.

Alexandro looked at me and asked, "What are you up to?"

"Nothing Daddy, nothing" I responded. He placed his hand on my thighs again and the surge it sent to me was simply amazing. Nectar was dripping heavy into my panties. I shifted; his hand crept closer to my inner thigh. He started to move his fingertips in circles sending goose bumps down my arms and thighs; I couldn't help but open my legs for his hands to explore more. He leaned over to kiss me, our tongues intertwining; the passion was evident.

My, I want him, I want him right now.

He pushed my panties to the side and whispered *"damn"* in my ear as he felt how soaked they were. He placed his fingertips onto my sweetness. Trust, if I were standing I would have fallen down because his touch made me light headed. One finger went completely in then out and straight to his mouth. He inhaled my essence before tasting it. He was driving me fucking insane. My legs were moving side to side with the same motion as earlier from my nervousness.

All passengers were aboard the plane, a voice told us to fasten our seatbelts, soon the take off. I wanted Alexandro more than ever.

I spoke softly in his ear, "How bout we take this to the bathroom? I want your tongue exploring every inch of my girl."

"Damn Boo," he was shocked, "for real here on the plane?"

"Yes, I don't want to wait anymore. I need it right now." I begged him "Daddy, I need to cum really bad." I proceeded to stand and straightened my dress and adjust my panties…

Now I'm standing and looking down, noticed his dick was standing to attention as he looked at me. He placed his hands on my legs as I began to move out of my seat. I was seducing him with my eyes, giving him a lustful look. I was begging for him to follow me into the bathroom. Since the plane was a small one there weren't any stewardesses at the back.

Wonderful, we can both be inside.

I looked back and saw Alexandro heading to the bathroom. I entered the bathroom and left it unlocked for him.

When he entered I was sitting on top of the sink with my panties in hand and my legs wide open. Alexandro let out a grunt as he entered.

"Damn Isabella you look fuckin hot," he said before

he got on his knees, placing his head between my legs. He started to kiss on my sweetness with little pecks. I arched my back hitting my head into the mirror. I waited for this for so long. He looked up and said "Isabella, this is about you. I want you to enjoy. I'm gonna take care of this pussy."

"Daddy," I whimpered…*mmmmm*. His hands spread the lips of my sweetness apart; my nectar dripping at a steady pace as he sucked on my 'pearl' making it extra hard. He ran his tongue up and down on my inner lips softly and slowly. Alexandro increased the rhythm; began to move faster and harder. Dipping his tongue into my wet pussy and swallowing my flow. *Damn*, I wanted to scream but didn't want to bring any type of attention to the back of the plane. I grabbed his head and slid closer on to his tongue and grinded my hips to the pulse of his tongue. "Aye, Daddy" I wailed. My legs started to shake.

I felt it coming on strong. I started breathing very hard crying out *"yes" "yes"* as the thunder was about to happen. I warned him "Papi…I'm going to cum."

He kept on moving faster, it excited him knowing he was about to bring me to pleasure. My entire body started to shiver. I pushed his head away so he could watch as I squirted into the sink. My entire body became weak at that very moment.

Alexandro looked on with amazement because he never experienced something like it before and said "Damn, I didn't know it was like that."

I giggled and said, "You made it like that...

Now I think I've fallen in love.

He giggled as he helped me off of the sink. My knees buckled as another orgasm hit me with nectar flowing down my thighs. Alexandro held me so I wouldn't fall.

We were facing each other; I leaned in and gave him a fierce kiss. There was a knock on the door. He answered, "Be right out." He helped me put my panties back on and said. "We'll finish this in Vegas, baby girl."

All I could say was, "Uh huh, we sure will." Alexandro rinsed his mouth, cleaning the dry cum off his face before we headed out.

The two of us couldn't have cared less if the whole plane knew what we had been doing. *Shit,* we both were satisfied for the moment. If someone had entered the bathroom they would definitely know what went down, because my essence was in the air.

Shower

Monica Martinez

Mike was a 6'1 215 lbs, brown skin Puerto Rican who wears his hair in cornrows. He wears a size twelve shoe, so ladies you already know what I was expecting. His body was immaculate, has an eight pack not even a six. The muscles on his body are just straight sick. The only thing is he is twenty two and I'm well, let's just say I'm old enough to be his mother. He came to clean my carpet. I had been eyeing him for some time. I was forward on numerous occasions with nothing to show for it. One day my forwardness finally paid off. Now I have him whenever he works for me.

He was upstairs in my shower.

I was in the next room undressing...

I entered the bathroom with just my high heels because I'm very short next to him. I am five feet, well, with heels I'm 5'3. I got into the shower, he turned around. I asked if he minded.

"No..." He stuttered, "...not at all."

I took the soap and lathered it to wash his broad back. I softly washed his back. He felt strong. I felt tiny next to him. I only weigh 113 lbs. When he turned completely around I washed his chest, admiring his strong young body. I was in complete heaven. I gasped as I ran my fingers up his washboard stomach. His member was long and thick and it wasn't even completely erect. Damn, he was packing ten or so inches.

He brought my face to his full lips then he kissed me on my forehead. I began touching him, exploring his body. His arms were big and strong. I worked my way down his stomach, pulled on his long pipe and began washing it. His dick started to get really hard. It was lovely like the rest of him. I licked my lips as I moved my hand up and down his shaft. He started to play with my hair telling me how lovely it is. It started to get wet from the shower and was getting wavy. I looked to him and said "You really turn me on." He took me and pushed me against the wall spreading my legs apart with his. He started to wash my body with the soap.

He moved his long fingers to my underworld and he was amazed how fat and juicy it was. My diamond started to throb. He looked down and saw I still had my heels on in the shower.

"Damn," he said with a laugh. "That's so fucking hot, having heels on in the shower."

He lifted one of my legs and entered me. I moaned with utter pleasure. He grabbed my hands and put them over my head onto the wall. He began pushing his long thick rod in and out of me. He proceeded to do it harder and harder. It felt good. I didn't want him to stop. I wanted to feel him all the way inside of me. I begged for him to give me more and more. He went deeper and deeper still, it hurt but it was a good hurt. I was enjoying him inside me; haven't had pleasure like this in a long while. He moved my body closer to his, grinded all the way inside of me.

I damn near fainted as I felt him all the way inside of my stomach. He was sucking on my neck, the feelings were crazy. I was there, about to reach my orgasm.

I screamed "I'm going to cum."

Just then he stopped, turned me around. He got down to his knees. He took my juiciness into his mouth. I exploded onto his tongue and down his throat. He just sent me into heaven. The water started to get colder. He rose and kissed me...

He carried me out of the shower to my bed. Here is where he showed me that young men never get tired and their energy can be a forever lustful adventure. His stamina was crazy. He took me to great pleasures and although I knew we could never have a relationship, it was good to feel like Stella. I got my groove back.

Falling

Monica Marthez

...*I* don't know when it happened. Don't know why it happened, but it happened. I fell in love with him. It wasn't supposed to happen, *I swear it wasn't.* He invaded my thoughts on the regular. The more we spoke, the more connected I became with him. I wasn't supposed to get caught up like this. I can't be in love with two men at the same time. I tried to convince myself it's nothing. We are just two people who had other situations we were dealing with. Each time we met for a secret rendezvous my feelings caught me off guard. Just laying in his arms before making love felt so right. We would just talk about different things going on in our lives, the kids, work, the news… catching up from not being able to physically see each other.

Somehow we got closer. I leaned on him more than I would lean on my husband. I would call him and ask him for his advice and vice versa. We were souls that should have met in a different life time. He was my soul mate. I knew it since the first time we made love. We were far away in a hiding spot where no one would even think to find us.

We met in Delaware. Tucked away in a hotel lusting and showcasing the very hunger we shared for each other. Our bodies formed as one, our hearts beating at the same pace. We never lost eye contact throughout our love making session.

The day I told him, was a Sunday morning. We both had a business expo we were attending in Chicago. I was staying at the Hyatt. He was further downtown staying with some family. We had originally made plans for him to stay with me the night before. But that wasn't possible. His family lived there. *Damn didn't they know how much I needed him?*

I had looked forward to this weekend. I had plans on making love to him through-out our evening together. I wanted to sleep in his arms. I wanted to awaken in the morning to his scent. I was disappointed when he told me

233

he couldn't come thru. It was then at that moment I realized my feelings were deeper for him than I ever intended. He had me hooked.

He was on his way to see me first thing in the morning. He told his family he had a business meeting at seven in the morning. We both didn't need to be at the convention center till twelve in the afternoon. It was perfect, only I had taken Tylenol PM to help me sleep that Saturday night; he texted me Saturday night. I was a zombie and couldn't fight the drowsiness off. I could barely read his text let alone respond to them.

Early Sunday morning my phone was ringing. It was him indicating he was on the subway heading to me. The meds were still in my system and I couldn't get it together. I just lay in the bed with my eyes closed. I was going back to sleep. Nonetheless, at seven in the morning I forced myself out of the bed. I took a shower and tried to get myself moving. I wanted to be alone with him all weekend. I got glimpses of him at the convention center and we even met a couple of times to talk. We snuck in a few kisses here and there and even some quick feels. My body was in need of his touch. I hadn't made love to him in about a month.

We live in two different cities and originally I thought it could work for me. I wouldn't get attached to him and the same would go for him. Well being so far away from each other only made us that much closer to one another. I found him in my thoughts on a regular basis. I could be washing laundry and I thought about him. How I would love to cook for him and have him come home to me after a long day's work. I could love him forever. He's fine, intelligent, has a nice big dick and knows how to work it. Let me not forget to mention his skills with the tongue. His main concern was keeping me sexually satisfied whenever were together. It's no wonder I fell for him.

Chauncey stands 5'11, and weighs 170 lbs. He's a mixture of White and African American, but somehow he looks like he's Spanish. His eyes are dark brown. He's a light skinned brother with wavy hair. He jokes and says he's got the good hair. He's so silly sometimes. His teeth are beautiful, straight and white. His lips are full, the minute he smiles, he lights up a room. He keeps in shape and I love that about him. His waistline is a straight V. His body is chiseled into a perfect mold in my eyes. Bulging muscles everywhere, even in his legs. The cologne he wears drives me crazy. It mixes with his chemistry and set's me on fire.

I stood in the shower hoping the cold water would wake my ass from the medicine. Twenty minutes later I found myself back in my bed, awaiting him with my eyes closed.

Not sure how much longer it was before he was knocking on my room door. He came in and I kissed him and crawled back into my bed. I told him I was still feeling woozy from the pills. He undressed, jumped in the bed naked and cuddled me. I felt his hardness pulsating on my back. We did our normal stuff, talked and God how I wanted to turn to him and say, *Chauncey I love you. I'm in love with you…*

…However, I'm not the type to lay my feelings on the line. I was mad at myself about last month. Chauncey came into town. I was going through some stuff which hit me close to home. I never cry in front of my husband because it's a sign of weakness. Yet I cried in Chauncey's arms.

In Chauncey's arms I felt safe. He was my missing piece. He placed soft kisses on my cheek then moved to the back of my neck and down my entire spine. Fuck meds or no meds I knew where it was gonna wind up.

Chauncey asked, "Melissa, are you okay?"

"Papi, I'm more than okay," was my response.

He turned me around and placed his lips on my second set of swollen slits. Mmmmm, the pleasures he was about to give me. I knew it was second to none. Chauncey knows all the right spots on 'her'. He drives me insane. He licked softly while holding my sweetness apart. The minute his tongue took a dive into my tunnel I screamed. The tidal wave approached so quickly gushing down into his mouth.

He drank my juice as if he was dehydrated. He didn't stop there. He moved to my 'pearl', flicking his tongue on it. I had to sit up to see what the hell he was doing to me. I loved the way he made me feel.

I screamed, "Papi Te amo!"

Soon as the words left my mouth I wanted to crawl away. It was great he didn't understand a word of Spanish. He didn't know what I was saying. Whew, lucky me he kept working his tongue down below. Chauncey I screamed over and over again as he continued to take me to pleasures. He was putting it on me, no doubt about it. Each time we got together it was more intense then our first session.

Once my body shivered beyond control, he moved his tongue up my stomach to my breasts. He placed his big hands on my tits, taking my brown nipples into his mouth and seducing me with his eyes.

The words slipped once again in Spanish, "Dame mas te amo…"

He looked at me as if he knew what I meant.

"Melissa, whatever you just said sounds so fucking sexy."

I reached for his manhood and stroked it. I wanted to feel him inside of me, making me complete. I hated myself at the moment for cheating on my loving husband. However, I loved Chauncey and there was no denying it.

Chauncey moved closer on me to give me all of him. *Damn* he fitted perfectly inside my 'girl'. The pressure of his weight on top of me, it turned me on even more. He moved slowly until his body completely covered mine. His kisses were deep and hot. I felt vulnerable and consumed with desire as he moved further inside. He breathed heavily into my ear whispering my name. He moved slowly and deliberately using his thighs to rock me side to side and open me wide.

He paused, eased up and put both hands under me pulling me closer to him. My legs straddled his hips. I screamed and moaned, overwhelmed with emotion. Ecstasy came quickly as he continued to stroke me with tenderness. I couldn't help myself.

I looked him in the eyes, "Chauncey te amo."

We were wild with desire, dripping wet with our passion and trembling with satisfaction. Chauncey came hard inside of me.

We lay still on the bed cuddling. It's so wrong yet it feels so right. I've fallen for him.

"Te amo Chauncey…" I whispered and fell asleep in his arms.

We were tucked away from the real world and in our own. I didn't want to leave him. I didn't even want to go back to the damn Convention center. We had commitments to other people and places, yet I wished we could just run away and never look back.

We were wide awake within the hour. I played with the hair on his chest as I leaned on him.

"You are a beautiful woman. I wish we could be like this forever."

Was he telling me he felt the same way?

"Melissa, this feels so right. I think if we met at a different time we would have been married to each other."

Damn, what do I do? What do I say to him?

Melissa, just tell him how you feel see if he feels the same way…?

He rose off the bed and headed to the shower. I was mad at myself because I was scared to be open on how I felt about him.

I wandered into the bathroom and called out his name, "Chauncey."

He looked at me through the shower glass, "Yes baby?"

Here it goes…

"Te amo means, I love you."

Chauncey looked at me and smiled.

"I love you too, Melissa."

I smiled as I entered the shower to join him. I get some more of his loving under the hot steamy water.

Naughty Girl
Monica Martinez

Sylvia's phone rang, it was eleven at night. She knew who was calling her. He said he would call her at exactly that time. She let the phone ring twice before she answered. She didn't want to appear too anxious. She met him about two weeks ago at an underground club in the city. He had a dark look about him. Andres was his name. He stood 5'11, had jet black hair that was pushed back. He had dark mysterious eyes. His eyes had the eyeliner look although he wasn't wearing any. He had a bronze complexion. Andres was desirable in Sylvia's eyes. Sylvia entered the club two weeks ago wearing her gothic look.

Sylvia stood 5'5. She weighed 135 lbs. She had long jet black hair. That night at the club she resembled Elvira. She put on her bodysuit girdle which pushed her waist in, making it smaller than her 25 inches. The girdle pushed her plump breasts, making her 34 B cup look more tantalizing. Her hips looked bigger than the 36 inches they were. She lined her sea blue eyes with lots of eye shadow and black eyeliner. She wore black lipstick then went over it with a lip gloss shine. Earlier in the morning she got a manicure and pedicure with matching black nail polish. She threw on her black garter belt with the matching fishnet stockings. Finishing the look she put on her black patent leather pumps. Satisfied with her look Sylvia smiled as she glanced in the mirror.

Her girlfriend Maria told her about an underground S&M club in the City. Not many people knew about it, you had to get on a list and getting on the list was a daunting task. Sylvia begged Maria to include her name as she always wanted to experience it at least once. Sylvia firmly believed if you haven't experienced every type of sex at least once, you weren't fully a woman. She lived by that law and always protected herself when she went on her bad girl nights as she called them.

That night she walked into the dark club, which was located in the lower east side of Manhattan. She walked through a long tunnel with red light bulbs. She could hear the music playing as she got closer to the doors. She heard R. Kelly's song Thoia Thong playing. She was asked for I.D., which she gave to the young pretty lady at the front door. She paid her fifty dollars to enter and left her email address. They informed her she was now a member and her entrance fee in the future would only be ten bucks.

The club was dark with green lights flashing. There were women on swings above, swinging and dancing to the music. Women dressed only in black fishnets were grinding on stripper poles in every corner of the club. Sylvia liked the scene and the music that was playing. Disturbia came on from Rihanna. She started to whine her body as she walked through the crowd. Men were immediately attracted to her and followed her with their eyes.

Sylvia made it to the bar, ordered a long island iced tea. She waited as the bar tender fixed her drink. That's when Andres appeared and pressed against her back. He whispered in her ear, "You're such a bad girl I'll buy that drink for you." Immediately Sylvia's body awakened with electricity.

She purred like a kitten as Andres turned her around with force.

She stared into his dark eyes first, then gave the rest of him the once over. He had a leather vest with the matching tight pants, which pressed against his massiveness. Sylvia bit her lip when she saw what he was working with. Andres was masculine, his chest rippled with muscles. Sylvia was pleasantly pleased with his defined looks and amazing body. It looked like she had found her boy toy for the night. Andres took her by the hand and led her to the dance floor. They danced to R. Kelly's, Move Your Body, like a snake by...

Sylvia shook her hips side to side moving only the lower portion of her body. She started to slither like a snake moving her tongue close to Andres's ear licking his earlobe. Andres was impressed. Although he frequented this club he never came upon such an intriguing young lady. Andres wanted to take her to one of the rooms downstairs and play with her.

He pressed his body closer to hers, grabbing her waist.

"Naughty little girl." He whispered in an ear.

She smiled giving him a devilish look. He kissed her lips with a slight peck. Sylvia smelled a citrus flavor from his mouth. He was turning her on with his dance moves and forwardness. She turned around pushing her boxy bottom on his manhood. She gyrated on him, making sure to awaken the bulge in his pants. Andres took his right hand and traced her boobs with his fingers. Sylvia's nipples instantly became erect. Andres wanted to punish this naughty girl by teasing her body to no end. They continued to dance as Usher's song; Love in this Club began...

Sylvia's body was filled with hunger and desire. Her flower needed to be watered. She wouldn't mind this tall mysterious stranger causing her flower to bloom.

Andres whispered, "I've never seen you here before?"

"Well, of course not, this is my first time. I'm a virgin to this particular scene."

Andres wanted to make her one of his disciples. He had many women under his control. He was going to bring a new one home to his flock. Andres grabbed her hand and led her towards the back of the club, down a flight of stairs.

Sylvia didn't mind following him. He had an aura about him which made you want to submit. He took her down to a dark basement filled with little rooms. Sylvia noticed the rooms didn't provide any privacy. Couples were having sex in the open and the pungent smell of sex streamed through the air. Sylvia took a deep breath and inhaled the tangy smells that flowed through the rooms. Her body was stimulated as she watched the different couples fucking. Andres found the room he had hoped wasn't taken and lead her to the bed.

The bed had straps on each of the four posts. He laid Sylvia down and strapped her legs first.

Sylvia said, "Oh… You're such a naughty boy."

Andres unfastened her body girdle and let her breasts loose. He was fascinated with her body as he helped her out of her girdle. Once it was off, he pushed her back onto the bed and strapped her wrists. Sylvia didn't know what he had in store for her. She was ready for whatever. She was eager for him to swarm her body. Andres' body had a husky scent to it. Sylvia took a deep breath of his aroma. It was making her pussy palpitate.

Andres took out a whip tickler; it had a feather on one end and a whip on the other. "This is what I use on the naughty girls."

Sylvia crooned with delight, "Dame Papi."

"Beg for it." He commanded.

He slapped her breasts with the whip softly.

"Mmmmm," She yelled out. "More. Give me more" She screamed.

He whipped her harder across her breasts making her

nipples harden. She squirmed with pleasure. She didn't experience this type of S&M, ever. The sting against her flesh exhilarated her body's senses. Her pussy juice fell into her wet black thongs dripping down her inner thighs.

Andres hit Sylvia again with the whip harder than before. She screamed as she felt the rush of her orgasm. The hitting seemed so provocative to Sylvia. She couldn't seem to get enough.

"You naughty girl…. You must be punished." Andres yelled.

Sylvia pleaded with Andres not to have any mercy on her.

Andres took the feather part and traced the welt he left on her body, soothing it before he gave her another hard slap. Sylvia screamed at the top of her lungs as her body exploded once again. Andres took the whip down to her pussy and bent to his knees. He inhaled the scent of her wet cherry. Satisfied with the fragrance below he took the whip and smacked the lips.

Sylvia thought she was going to lose control, damn she couldn't even grab at him because she was bound to the bed. The blood flow running through her veins made the temperature of her body hotter. He was taking her body to a whole different level of ecstasy. He continued to punish her until her body shook beyond control and she yelled she couldn't take anymore. Her body was exhausted from the amount of orgasms he gave her. She needed to take a break. Andres stopped, walked around to her face, lowered his lips down to hers letting his tongue explore the insides of her mouth. Her body was drenched in sweat and there were welts over her breasts and down to her thighs, once unbound she was sure she wouldn't be able to stand.

Andres loosened her bonds, helped her to her feet and dressed her again. He took her back to the main floor of the club. He asked for her number and disappeared into the night like a vampire. Sylvia was in a daze from the sensations he gave her. She decided her *Naughty Girl* night was a rap and headed back to her apartment. After showering she noticed the welts on her skin. Just looking at them made her think about the night. She got excited all over again.

Her phone rang. She let her answering machine do its work. It was Andres leaving her a message telling her "This is your master, Andres. I'm going away. I will call you back in two weeks. Naughty Girl, I want to see you upon my return as you are now one of my disciples."

Sylvia smiled.

She put lotion on her welted body.

Thug Passion

Chante Graham

There he was 5'8, 160 pounds. He looked like Morris Chestnut with a body like LL cool J. This man was gorgeous. I was getting off the train at my usual stop, my usual time and I always saw him walking his pit bull as I had to pass the park everyday on my way home. Everything with me was so predictable; if someone wanted to kill me it would be very easy. See, I'm not spontaneous at all. I could be sort of an introvert.

I'm single and have been celibate for the last three years. After my ex did me dirty I swore off men until I could get my head together. My toys and the internet keep me busy but after three years a girl could start getting a little crazy. I found myself always on edge, how can you go from getting it on a regular to using dildos and being in sex chat rooms with total strangers. It's really a lonely life and I'm sick of it. I just want to escape, get out of the box and experience life. I'm thirty three years young, I have a short haircut and my hair is naturally curly and dusty blonde. I stand around 5'6, 34C waist a size 27. I have curves but I'm so shy at times I don't want to show them. My ex-husband said he needed more spice in his life and he said I was boring him. He asked me for a divorce, later I found out he was cheating with his personal trainer. I don't think I stepped in a gym in five years because of that. I was really depressed after the breakup and I have been living in a shell for the last three years. I vowed the next man I fell in love with I would be more adventurous in and out of the bedroom.

Today was different, I felt like I needed a change and damn I needed some dick and I don't mean a rubber one either. I mean a real hard penis, it didn't matter the size I didn't care. Some women are fixed on it having to be this size or that size, this girth this length. God made man in all shapes and sizes just like women. What if men discarded us based on the size of our breasts or ass, it's really not fair. Thus I'm walking my usual route on a hot August day.

I have on a white strapless dress with white sandals, my hair curly. There he is again definitely not my type at all but like I said I was thinking outside of the box today. My horoscope read; *don't let unexpected situations throw you.* Who knows, perhaps he could be my knight in shining armor.

He was wearing a black doo-rag with black Levis and a white tee. Oh my God he had a great upper body it was showcased through his t-shirt. It looked like he worked out daily. Just looking at him I began to get moist. I decided to say something; hell I know he sees me everyday too.

"Hi that's a pretty dog you have" I sounded stupid I'm thinking in my head.

"It's a pit, thanks, what's your name pretty?"

"Jackie…" I tried to sound seductive.

"I love your haircut, its sexy ma".

"Thank you." I cracked a little smile. Shit, I needed a drink for this. I'm not good at flirting. I need flirting for dummies.

"Why are you so shy?"

"I don't know. I' m just not good at this kind of stuff"

"What stuff? Shit, you look good. Any man would be crazy not to notice you. I see you every day you get off the 5:25, Q train and you never miss a day of work."

I laughed in my heart because he noticed me.

"Why don't you sit a minute so we can talk"?

He chained his dog, Mott to the bench as we sat down.

"No one will bother us with Mott here we can get to know each other without any interruptions."

Mott sat still, growling every now and then when a child ran by, but for the most part he behaved.

"So Ms. Lady, tell me about your self?"

He took off his doo-rag and had so many waves I was getting sea sick. His teeth pearly white and he had beautiful hazel eyes. They were amazing. I wasn't going to tell him about my past. I didn't want to him to judge me or think I was hard up.

"Do you like Italian ice, I bet cherry is your favorite flavor?"

It wasn't but I happily agreed. He summoned the ice guy to make us two cherry Italian ices. I thought to myself, *he is so romantic.* I could see it in his eyes. Next to the chat rooms this was the most action I've had with a live man in three years.

As he undressed me with his eyes I started to tingle.

"I'm 33. I work as a Chiropractor in midtown."

"Can I ask who your favorite author is?" That took

me by surprise because he didn't look like the reading type, if there is such a thing. I admit I can be so rigid at times. Despite looking like a thug he was very well spoken.

"Well my favorite author is George Bernard Shaw, what about yourself?" "Mark Twain is my favorite, but I really love Pablo Neruda."

There is substance to this man and he is sexy as hell. His name was Raiden. "Are you single Jackie?"

"Yes."

"Why? You are so beautiful. You should have a ring on that finger."

"Bad timing I guess, what about you?"

"Still waiting for, Ms. Right..."

"Maybe you just found her." I said rather boldly. I felt sexy as hell all of a sudden. He was invoking confidence in me by the way he complimented me. He made me feel beautiful.

"You are taken in the net of my music, my love and my nets of music are wide as the sky, my soul is born on the shore of your eyes of mourning, in your eyes of mourning the land of dreams begin" He spoke to me so poetically. Poetically for someone who just took off a doo-rag that is.

"That was beautiful yours?" I asked.

"No Pablo's."

We laughed.

My pussy was throbbing while we sat and chatted. All I wanted him to do was kiss me. As far as I was concerned I knew everything I wanted to know at this moment. Nothing else mattered.

"Motts hungry, would you mind coming with me to feed him. Then maybe we can grab a bite to eat?" I didn't know this man from Adam but his eyes made me feel safe. There was calmness to them. Somehow I trusted him. "Don't worry I'm not a rapist or criminal. I'm sure you sized me up already."

I just had this dumb look on my face. He was right…

Thus I used my cell phone and texted my friend Jennifer. Just to let her know where I was going in the event I was never to be seen again. He lived about five minutes away in a loft building. In my thirty three years I've never done anything like this, but if you don't live life you never know what could have been. This was a life outside of the box day for me.

We walked three long flights of steps to his abode. I was sweating bullets by the time we reached his floor. His loft was beautiful and he had lovely artwork all over, and built in book cases with at least a thousand books, and mosaic columns around the loft. He had a beautiful red leather soda, a pool table and a Ms. Pac-man video game unit. Compared to my quarter sized studio, I felt like I was in a mansion.

"I love your place."

"Thanks. I have a roommate but she is on the road right now."

Whoa.

Wait one minute....

He did say she right? In spite of that I didn't ask any questions. It wasn't my business at this point.

Mott went to eat in his little corner. Raiden was an artist. I walked around the loft to admire his artwork. As I looked at one picture of a beautiful woman with a tear running down her cheek, I said to myself, I've seen this picture before at the MOMA? I looked closer and it was autographed R. Stone. I'm like hell no this can't be the famous artist? I kept looking around while he was upstairs taking a shower. Every painting was autographed R. Stone. I couldn't believe it, I was in love with this man I thought was a thug; he was actually a famous artist. God blessed me this afternoon.

"Oh my God Raiden, is this your work?" I blurted when he came back downstairs.

"Who did you think R. Stone is? A renaissance woman like yourself I thought you would have recognized my pieces"?

"I know now. I recognized the one with the woman with the tear running down her face."

He was smiling from ear to ear.

"Beautiful." I simply stated. "It's beautiful."

We stared at each other for about two minutes. I got lost in his eyes.

"I'm going to be real with you. I know you have been hurt in the past. I can feel your spirit, you have a genuine heart and baby I'm not here to break it but to mend that hole in it."

I melted and my heart felt heavy. Love at first sight this may be it, in five years of marriage, I've never felt these feelings.

I felt boldness and said, "Kiss me."

He leaned in and kissed me so softly and passionately. He started working his tongue around my mouth so deeply I was ready to explode. As we kissed he grabbed me close to him, our bodies meshed together as though he was scared to let me go. We kissed for what seemed like an eternity.

He asked me to pleasure him with some ice, I obliged because I always wanted to do that. When he came back from the fridge with the ice, I did something even bolder, extremely bolder. I pulled down his pants. He seemed shocked but the shock only lasted as long as it took for me to take his dick out of his boxers. I went to my knees and used the ice. Did I mention I started sucking his dick?

I put the ice in my mouth and sucked his manhood. I didn't drop the ice once. The coldness of the ice mixed with the hardness of his dick, made me erupt. The way he moaned sent chills down my spine.

The foreplay was incredible and I anticipated feeling him inside of me. I tasted his sweetness mixed with the water from the ice cubes in the warmth of my mouth, it tasted like lemonade. Sweet, cold and I didn't need any sugar. Impressed on him I was. He took me to new heights that hot August evening, took me atop a skyscraper.

We both went to the floor. I put my arms around his columns with my ass facing him. He proceeded to lick the back of my legs as he made his way to my hidden tunnel. Yes we both got naked. I don't even remember how. Whether he undressed me or we undressed each other. It just happened.

He spread my legs apart as far as they could go as his

tongue worked its way up my middle. I thought I was going into convulsions the way I was shaking.

"Baby, don't be scared. I won't hurt you." With those words my sweetness erupted from between my legs and dripped on the floor, an orgasm so powerful 1,025 days of love juice that hasn't been burst. "Damn baby," He uttered before he licked my juice from my pussy. Then he started licking it from off the floor. He went back to my middle. I was stomach first, stretched out and didn't move much then I started squirming. His tongue started slithering around the outsides of my walls, his tongue moved to the motion of my body.

I wanted this dude and he knew. He held my ass with a firm hand, used the other to prop me up. He slid his manhood in me doggy style pumping the shit out of me while I was on my stomach first. Then he stood me on shaking legs.

We were standing. I held onto thin air, didn't know how I managed not to fall. I was so tight after three years I know he loved it. He fucked me good. I bent down to touch the floor. I was in the zone, doing shit like I'd been getting fucking on the regular.

Each thrust became harder and harder as he pumped into me. My pussy totally enlarged as his dick filled it. I was cumming harder than I ever did in my life. I let out a long moan I couldn't hold back anymore. His dog got riled by me, started barking to my moaning.

I erupted all over his dick. He quickly pulled out and pushed me to my knees. He wanted me to suck all of his juices out. And that is what I did. It came out like a hydrant, like he hadn't had sex as long as I hadn't. I didn't choke. I took it. It tasted good as it filled my mouth. I played with his babies oaring them with my tongue before I swallowed it all.

Some of the remnants of his cum were still left on his dick. I licked it all the way down to his balls.

Raiden was going crazy at this point. He was totally transfixed and completely satisfied. We lay on the bare floor afterwards, cuddled in each other's arms. I lived outside the box today. It felt wonderful. This was thug passion for real…

"One…"

Sasha

Alexandra Castilo

*D*amn, it's been a long cruel work week, however, it was a Friday night and I was going out with Vicky. Vicky is my best friend, we grew up together and we tend to have the same taste women! Yes, you heard me correctly. I am a straight Lesbian. Well, they actually call my type a lipstick lesbian. My name is Sasha and I stand 5'2, and weigh 125 lbs. I have long black hair that goes way past my ass. I'm a hot Latina, lesbian. I got curves that could make a man lose their mind, once they realize I'm strictly for the women that is. Most men say it's a shame. I don't care. I'm not interested in them and never will be bottom line.

Vicky and I made plans to go hit one of our usual spot in Manhattan. I told her I would meet her behind around eleven or so, because I had made plans with this cute girl named Angie for dinner.

I had met Angie about a week ago at a friend's birthday party. She has a girlfriend who is away at college. I normally don't date a person in a relationship. However, there is a first time for everything, especially since Angie said she finds me interesting. I have been single for about two months and if I'm being honest I was feeling extremely horny.

I arrived home at seven. I only had an hour to get ready for Angie. She was scheduled to pick me up at exactly eight. I had to rush and find an outfit that screamed, *fuck me baby!* I looked in my closet, because I know I had the perfect outfit somewhere in there. I found the little black tube top dress I never wore. I needed to try it on and hot damn, I'd fuck me if I wasn't me. I felt sexy and the dress fitted perfectly on my tits. They really meant little when they made the dress. I was gonna have to be careful because if I bend over the whole world will see my nice plump booty. Yes I have back; my measurements are 34B, 23, and 38.

This dress doesn't require a bra, which in my mind was absolutely perfect. If the air conditioner was working properly my nipples would become visibly erect. I threw on my Steve Madden 4' inch black pumps. I had my long black hair straightened earlier in the day.

It was time to put on some make-up and gloss my full plump lips. I sprayed perfume on every inch of my body, especially on my black thongs. I knew I was going to get some pussy come hell or high water. I grabbed my purse, my cell phone and looked at the clock. Its eight o'clock on the dot. I knew Angie would be downstairs waiting on me.

As it was planned, there she was in her black Acura. I jumped in her car and kissed her on the lips saying, "Hello."

She looked at me as if she had never been kissed by another woman before. I laughed in her face "What's wrong?"

She just smiled "Thank you for coming out to dinner with me tonight." "The pleasure is all mines, Angie," was the response, followed by a chuckle. I liked Angie because she was simple and cute. She wasn't one of these complicated women like me. I have to get all dolled up to go anywhere. But not her, she's all T-shirts and Jeans, simple.

We arrived at LezDine for dinner. Yes, the name say's it all. It's a Lesbian owned restaurant in the Village. I had wanted to go badly. Every single lesbian raved about this place. They said the food and service were great. Not to mention there are a lot of beautiful woman and I could never let a beautiful woman pass me by.

The restaurant had Sex appeal; it looked like an Old Bordello. We sat for dinner. When the waitress came to our table Angie ordered for me. I thought it was completely sexy. She began to talk about work, college and of course her girlfriend. She commented about how much she wished she was not in a relationship and how she found herself very attracted to me. At that point in time I knew it wouldn't go any further. It would be only dinner and nothing more. It was apparent she was in love. When dinner ended I told her I was going to meet my girlfriend at Clouds, a gay club in midtown. I extended the invitation to her. She didn't decline. Angie called a few of her friends and invited them to Clouds as well. They were going to meet us there...

We arrived at the club at exactly eleven. I was thrilled to see my home-girl Vicky waiting for me with my favorite drink in hand *Vodka Cranberry*. The club was definitely the place to be, there were beautiful women all over the place. Angie decided she was going her separate way which was perfect cuz it was time for me to mingle!

There were all types of Lesbian's available. Vicky and I like two little lesbians in a candy store. I was standing at the bar when I spotted a beautiful blonde. She was 5'4 had long straight hair, and was curvy. From where I was standing I could see she had a nice big rack on her with a small waste. Damn, she had a nice fat ass as well. When I see something I like I must always have it. I asked the bartender to send her a drink on me. The bartender placed the drink in front of her and informed her I sent it over. The sexy blonde head looked over at me and greeted me with a smile.

Fuck she was hot and sexy. Yummy I just wanted to eat her up.

I told Vicky about what I wanted to do to the beautiful blonde.

Vicky laughed. "You're such a Pimp Sasha."

We cracked up and headed to the dance floor.

I started dancing all the while flirting with the blonde at the bar. After six songs I was feeling hot and was in need of a drink to freshen up. I walked to the bar where the blonde head was and order a drink.

I got her attention and introduced myself. "Hi. I'm Sasha."

She smiled. "Hi. I'm Crystal."

"Would you like another drink?" I asked.

Crystal said "Yes but I got this round."

I thought to myself *round hmm, that means she wants to have more than one drink in my company.*

I smiled at her. I shook my head, sure.

We started talking. She told me she was from Queens and she lived with a roommate. She recently broke up with her girlfriend and she informed me she was a Police Officer. I continued to flirt and tell her how much I love a woman in uniform.

"Well, as for me, I live and work in the city for a marketing firm. I broke up with my horrible girlfriend two months ago and ever since I have been going on date's nothing major."

While talking to Crystal, I noticed she had the most beautiful eyes I have ever seen. Her eyes were a Gold color with very long eyelashes; her nose was cute and small. Her lips were nice and juicy. I wanted to kiss her badly. She was making me horny. She had on a button down shirt, the first few were unbutton. You could see the shape of her beautiful full 36C size breast. I asked her if she wanted to dance. She agreed. I grabbed her hand and we hit the dance floor.

While we were dancing I could feel her breasts on mine. I started to get hot as her perfume filled my nostrils. I pushed closer to her body.

She was yummy.

I wanted to eat and lick her right on the dance floor. She looked at me as if she was reading my mind.

Crystal asked. "Sasha would you like to go outside for some fresh air?"

Glad she was able to read my body language.

Once we got outside we began to kiss, it was obvious we were attracted to one another. Her lips tasted delicious I wanted her. Crystal kissed my neck as she pressed her body against mine. We began to kiss more passionately.

"Crystal," I asked. "Would you like to go somewhere more private?"

She quickly responded, "Yes. I would love to."

She said her car was up the block. We walked holding hands. Once we reached her vehicle, we jumped in quickly. Before the key was even in the ignition, she placed one hand on my leg and started to move slowly to my pussy. I opened my legs for her. We were gonna get busy and there was no question about it. Her hand began to rub on my wet second set of lips. I was dripping. I couldn't wait for her to fuck me.

She slipped two fingers in my deep dark tunnel. I felt like a virgin, it was almost as if I never had been fucked before. She was making me hot and boiling to the point of no return...

Fuck it, I took my dress off and let my tits fall.

"Damn Sasha," Crystal smiled. "You are beautiful."

I unbutton her shirt to reveal her big breasts. I place her breasts one by one in my mouth sucking on her nipples while she continued to finger fuck my shaved pussy. I unbutton her jeans and placed my hand inside of her panties. She also had a shaved pussy and it was dripping nectar. I slipped two fingers into her hole. Crystal began to moan as I move down pushing her pussy to my face. I placed my tongue in her sweetness and taste her juices. *Damn she tasted as good as she looked.*

I slide my tongue all through her slits and began to suck on her clit. She was moaning like crazy, pushing my head into her pussy. She yelled, begging me to fuck her harder. I gave her three fingers and fucked her pussy real good. Her body began to shiver. I knew she was about to climax while she was riding my face.

She screamed, "Harder... fuck me... harder."

I slid one finger inside of her backdoor, while continue

to eating her out with my three fingers fucking her. Her body began to move faster as my fingers kept going in and out of her pussy and ass.

I sucked on her clit till I felt her pussy contract. Her tidal wave gushed inside of my mouth. I drank all of her nectar. I got aroused from watching her. I was ready to cum.

I took my fingers out of her and adjusted her chair all the way down. I needed more room. I spread her legs apart and then I got on top of her. We were clit to clit, rubbing, pussy fucking and moaning to each other.

"Fuck me, Fuck me..."

She had me so excited. I came. The fluids within me dripped down to her pussy. We were kissing each other after my climax till she turned me around and paid a visit to my girl down south, licking what remained.

Damn! Crystal was going to be my girl. I was going to make sure of it. It was time to take this back to my place and have a repeat of the evening.

Foreign Escapade

story provided by Tamika Peters

Carlos was scheduled to pick up his wife at the airport at exactly five o'clock. She had been away for yet another week. He wanted to talk to her about these trips. Married for about five years, he was getting more suspicious about her frequent business trips and emergency office meetings. Carlos loved his wife and she never gave him a reason to question the trust he had for her, but nowadays she was always leaving, always had something to do. There had been times where he would call for hours straight and just get the voicemail. He admired his wife, at thirty five years old she was at the top of her game.

She was the founder of a prestigious financial consulting firm and in a class of her own, being the first Hispanic woman to run the most successful firm in the industry. Annabel stood 5'6", was 140 lbs with an olive complexion. Having origins from Brazil, she had an exotic beauty which was admired from men and women alike. Her sandy hazel eyes were so memorizing, strangers would stop her on the street just to speak with her.

Annabel spotted Carlos the minute she walked out of arrivals, pleased to see him and hoped the guilt wasn't written all over her face. She waved as she waited for her luggage. Annabel loved Carlos but she had demons that she continued to fight within herself. This whole marriage was becoming more of a chore than a committed relationship. Their lifestyle and sex life had become routine and stale. This trip had done her justice and was just what she needed, some excitement.

After successfully closing a multi-million dollar deal, she had an ample amount of free time. So she decided to tour the country, hell, she was always hearing stories about how Europeans were so open and sexually inhibited. She wanted to experience it for herself. The people were so friendly; it was hard to believe that she was actually visiting the country, by herself. She had a map and was touring interesting places and landmarks. That was how she met Michael. She was lost looking for a well known restaurant, just focusing on her map trying to pinpoint where she was. She bumped into him.

"Uh excuse me, I'm sorry to bump into you. I'm lost, trying to figure out where I was exactly."

"Oh, no, excuse me" He told her with a slight grin. Their eyes locked. Instantly the inner fire she thought had burned out was smoldering as was the rest of her body.

He stood about 6'3," was 220lbs of pure muscular strength; his complexion was like hers but a deeper copper tone. He was dressed very conservatively, wearing dark slacks and a button down shirt, but she saw through the clothes all his cuts and ripples.

"Excuse me miss, miss…?" he asked.

"Uh-uh…I-I'm sorry," She couldn't even get her thoughts together to speak without stuttering. She was mesmerized by him, like other people are with her. If she didn't have any panties on, her juices would have run down her legs, she was that taken away by him. "Oh. I'm so sorry, my name is Annabel Padilla. I'm visiting from the states. And you are?"

"I'm Micheal Encarna, I'm also a visitor but I come here often, at least three to four times a year. I live in Brazil."

Brazil, she thought, I bumped into a Brazilian in Europe.

"I was born there, I still have family there, where are you from?" She asked. He paused to reveal the most beautiful smile she had ever seen.

He didn't answer but he did say, "Why don't we take this conversation to the restaurant you were looking for and get to know each other over...?"

She was so enthused she blurted, "Okay…" before he could finish the sentence.

At the restaurant, they had a wonderful conversation. It had been a long time since she enjoyed such a conversation without talking business. He intrigued her, not just physically but mentally as well. At the end of their lunch, he suggested they meet later for a night on the town. She agreed without hesitation. They exchanged numbers and went on their merry way. Annabel was on cloud nine for the reminder of the day; she couldn't wait to go on her date. She thought about her husband and felt a little guilty, but she figured "I'm in a completely different country and what he doesn't know won't kill him."

Later that evening they had dinner by the seashore. Annabel was in such awe with the view; a few times she stopped eating just to take in the scenery. Micheal was such an intelligent man who spoke with such mannerism. However, from time to time Annabel tuned out what he was saying. She saw his lips moving but heard no sounds. She was fantasizing about how his luscious his lips would feel on her throbbing nipples. The thought alone made her nipples harden and since she was wearing a very sheer silk shirt showcasing her firm 34C breasts, it wasn't easy to hide. She was trying to focus on their conversation but her fantasies were taking over her thoughts. She kept crossing her legs because her swollen slits were distracted. She was so glad dinner was finally over, not because she didn't enjoy it. It was fantastic, but it was torture to be so close to an attraction and not be able to do anything about it.

After dinner, they went dancing, at one of the hippest clubs in town. The atmosphere was sexy and the music was blaring. Annabel and Micheal sat for a few minutes enjoying a drink.

"I like coming here when I visit." He told her after a sip. "The people seem so free just enjoying the moment, despreocupado, you know…"

Annabel nodded in agreement. She was taking in the whole scene. The club was dimly lit with neon disco lights enhancing the dance floor. Hanging from the ceiling, were metal cages that held couples doing erotic movements with each other. It was like visual foreplay for Annabel. She watched with anticipating eyes. "I know you don't see this in the States" Michael continued.

"I wish I could" giggled Annabel. "It's sexually arousing; it's like watching live porn."

Micheal was happy to know that Annabel was having a good time. From the moment he saw her, Micheal wanted her badly. He met beautiful women all the time and knew how to keep his composure. The deejay started to play salsa, interrupting his thoughts.

"Would you like to dance?" he asked.

"Absolutely, I love salsa" she replied in answer.

They headed to the dance floor Annabel began to swing her hips seductively, grinding her behind on his crotch. He immediately became hard. He followed her lead holding her by her waist, moving his waist against her round plump behind. Drunken with lust Annabel turned around to face him, she explored his mouth with her sweetened tongue. They shared a passionate kiss which sent chills down both their bodies. Still grooving to the music, their hands began caressing each other. His fingers ran across her perky breasts and her nipples stiffened.

She wanted to fuck him there on the dance floor. She guided her hands down to his pants, rubbing his cock. She was so impressed with his member. She couldn't take her hands off. She fumbled with his zipper for a few minutes until she got it open. She wanted to actually feel him without the barrier of clothes. She wanted to feel his manhood raw, in the flesh.

Aye Dios Mios, thought Annabel.

The blood flow was reaching a boiling point throughout her body. She damn near forgot they were still on the dance floor but nonetheless she really didn't care. Leaving his zipper open, Annabel turned around directed his hands underneath her flowing skirt. He outlined her ass with his hands and needed no directions to find her hidden wet treasure. The fact she was wearing crotch-less underwear, made it very accessible.

His fingers surveyed her saturated walls, it pulsated around his fingers and it excited him to the next level.

She leaned closer to his fingers and started whining her hips on them. Her womanly sap was dripping down his hands, he couldn't resist so he inserted another finger into her. Although, they were discreet with their actions, the chemistry was so intense between them that nearby couples slowed down to observe what they were doing. Micheal tactfully pulled out his hardened rod and slyly placed it in her moist opening. Still grinding her body against him, she felt him enter. She instantly gushed all over him. She worked her pussy against his throbbing member, taking all of him in.

An attractive woman was dancing close by them was eyeing the intense interaction between the two and unconsciously started massaging her breast while swaying to the instrumental beats. She smoothly grazed her way over so she could face Annabel. Annabel was in such ecstasy, it took her quite a few minutes to realize the sexy woman was staring at her. The moment their eyes locked, Annabel couldn't help but to be instantly attracted to this striking woman.

This beauty stood about 5'5", was 130lbs heavy, with curves that gave Jennifer Lopez a run for her money. She wore a form fitting pastel dress that hugged her assets perfectly. Her long auburn hair complimented her emerald eyes. She moved closer to Annabel.

Although Annabel had never been with a woman, sexually, her body was yearning for this mysterious lady. While Micheal rocked her middle section, Annabel bent over a little more. She wanted to showcase her bare breast to the woman. The gorgeous stranger gracefully danced her way closer and began running her fingers through Annabel's hair. She softly glided her fingertips along Annabel's neck and worked her down to her breast. She gently pinched her nipples while placing a delicate kiss on Annabel's glossy lips. Micheal finally realized what the two women were doing in front of him and his cock began to engorge more in Annabel's swollen walls. Annabel felt her walls expanding and knew Micheal was just as aroused as she was. The trio was moving very closely to each other with Annabel getting the best of both worlds. She was passionately kissing this woman while having her second pair of lips getting pounded by a thick juicy pole.

The woman's tongue tasted like syrup and she worked Annabel's mouth like she was about to pour all her maple down her throat. The thought alone took Annabel to a place she had never been to before much less the actual action. It was like having an out of body experience, the sheer thrill of having two gorgeous people touching, invading and conquering her.

"Oh awww, Annabel…" Micheal whispered in her ear, "My cock wants to rip you open, in the worst way, give me that fucking pussy."

He continued to ride her like a horse. The raunchy talk only heightened Annabel's exhilaration. She felt like she was gonna explode. Her pussy was talking real loud to his cock.

If it wasn't for the blasting music playing through the speakers, they would have heard her melody, "Ummm…" seeped out of her mouth between her kisses with the stranger. She wanted to know this foreigner's name but her words couldn't match her thoughts and at this point she wasn't even going to try. She just wanted to appreciate the moment.

The woman panted as if she was reading Annabel's mind but didn't want to reveal her identity. The woman tenderly cupped her breasts, released her lips from Annabel and gradually moved her mouth to where her hands were. Like a domino effect the onlookers were having their own trysts on the dance floor. One couple decided to take their private session into a very public manner and began to engage in rough sex, exposing all their nakedness for all to see. Still sucking on her breast, the woman released her hands and boldly moved them between Annabel's legs.

She knew Micheal was fucking her and she wanted to feel the wetness coming from Annabel's pussy. She placed her clit between her two fingers and made circular motions with it. She tugged at it moving further down her slits to feel Annabel's lips hugging Micheal's rod. Mimicking Annabel's v-spot she followed their rhythm and added an extra beat of her own against their bodies. Annabel slowly moved the woman's head to her face and licked her lips the same way she had massaged her clit. Annabel wanted to feel the softness of this woman's body so she held her by her hips and grabbed her luscious ass. Annabel maneuvered her hands under this strangers dress and began rubbing her bare shaven pussy. The stranger's womanhood was so enlarged that it felt like a mini pillow folded in half. It excited Annabel to feel her. She inserted her fingers in her and began finger fucking her swollen muscles.

Micheal was enjoying every minute of this private show. He wanted to remain calm but the fiery demonstration had him going wild. He could no longer contain his flowing soldiers and he released his hot liquid inside Annabel.

She felt the hot lava shooting into her tunnel and she began squirting juices of her own. Not missing a beat, she started rubbing the woman's clit intensely hard until her hands were just as drenched as her pussy.

"Oh yeah, I'm cumming yeah-h-h-h, baby…" The strange woman was out of breath. She was reaching her peak with Annabel's magic touch. With all three reaching their climax, all parties were satisfied. They had intentions of having a great time at the club but this was the cherry on top. After catching her breath, the mystery woman pulled down her dress.

"That was great Honey. Hope to see you around." She told Annabel. With that she spun around and walked off the dance floor.

A little taken back from her forwardness, Annabel turned to Micheal and asked if he knew her. He replied he saw her a few times before, but he didn't have the pleasure of actually knowing her. These Europeans are serious about getting their freak on, thought Annabel. But who was she to complain, she was more than content with her little freak fest. Now she had something to remember for years to come. Although it would have been nice to get to know this stranger a little better, she figured that's probably what made the whole encounter so much sexier, the mystery of it all. The atmosphere was filled with bodily fragrances, the room looked more like a swingers' club than a dance club, it made Annabel blush.

"Annabel, Annabel…" Carlos said as he grabbed hold of her arm, "Are you alright? You've been staring at your luggage for about twenty minutes or so." Annabel jumped and looked Carlos in the eyes.

"Y-yes, Micheal…?" She stuttered out of her mouth.

"Michael…." Carlos yelled. "Who the hell is that?"

She didn't realize how long she was daydreaming and her thoughts were scattered all over the place.

Awww shit, what am I gonna do? Annabel thought to herself. Annabel just realized the dilemma she had gotten herself into.

Carmen

Chante Graham

*I*t was a regular Friday night like any other. My girlfriend Carmen and I were going out for drinks at our usual spot in Midtown. Carmen is gorgeous, 5'7, 120 pounds 36D's with an olive skin tone and jet black long hair. She is the envy of so many women because she is gorgeous. We go way back, been friends since elementary school, have been friends for almost twenty years. Not too many people can say that. I love Carmen and she loves me. I am an average chick nothing spectacular. I don't have the sex appeal like Carmen but I think I'm still cute. I'm 5'5, 128 pounds and I'm around a 34C, with dusty blonde hair and green eyes.

We moved to New York City after being raised in Chicago as kids. Carmen landed a great job in a consulting firm and I was in law school about to take the bar soon. We dated men who were interesting to us and good looking. We had the same taste in everything. Carmen called me around six o'clock to meet at the Living Room in the W Hotel for drinks.

When we got there the place was quiet. Thus we were able to get a seat on one of the couches.

"Melissa, I had such a hard week. My boss stresses me the fuck out."

"I know what you mean girl but shit it's the weekend we can let our hair down."

After a couple of drinks we were feeling no pain, a couple of cute hunks came to talk to us.

"You ladies are beautiful are you sisters?" One of them asked.

"No, we just the best of friends" Carmen told the dude.

They started paying for drinks and things were becoming more interesting. One of them asked if we ever kissed a girl.

Carmen said, "I always wanted to."

I looked at her to see if she was serious. She was. She didn't even crack a smile. She sparked something in me.

Secretly, I had a crush on Carmen so bad I always wanted to eat her pussy. I knew it smelled and tasted delicious.

"Melissa," Carmen worded, "Don't you want to kiss me?"

I was like what the fuck? This can't be happening...

Meanwhile, the two assholes just stood there and gawked at us.

"Not here baby, let's go." Melissa told Carmen. I said that to dismiss the guys more than anything else. But I was still curious about Carmen.

We paid our tab and left those jerks sitting at the bar. We hopped in a yellow cab and went to my place. I lived on the lower east side.

"Carmen was you serious back there?"

"Hell yea I always wanted to feel a woman's lips on mine."

"Carmen," I asked with all out boldness "Would you kiss me?"

Carmen leaned over in the cab and grabbed the back of my head. She pulled me in to her and stuck her tongue in my mouth with such force. We kissed passionately. My pussy totally erupted all over with just one touch from Carmen. I couldn't believe this was happening. Carmen had a tongue ring that teased my mouth as we kissed. That shit felt so fucking good, all I could do was moan. I stuck my hands up Carmen's dress to feel if she was creaming and she was.

"Ma this shit feels so good I can't wait to taste it" I told her.

"Melissa I swear I wanted to stick my tongue down your throat for the last five years."

"Me too Carmen, you are so beautiful. I know you taste like Hershey kisses."

The cab driver couldn't get his eyes off of us through the rearview mirror we saw him gawking like a dog in heat. He probably had his dick out for all we knew.

We pulled up at my condo and kissed all the way to the door. I didn't know who would be the aggressor but I knew I wanted to fuck Carmen with my strap-on. Of course she didn't know I had one.

After we reached my apartment, I went to take a shower and slip into a sexy nightgown. When I came back Carmen was in her birthday suit looking luscious as ever. Her perfect breasts were looking at me. Her nipples were the eyes. Her butterfly tattoo right above her pussy was driving me crazy.

"Ma can I lick that butterfly?"

"Come on baby, what you got for me"?

"Lay down" I told her.

Carmen immediately obliged.

I got on top of her and we kissed passionately until we were both creaming. I cupped her breasts in my mouth as I sucked on her nipples one by one, until they became totally hard and erect. She loved it. I wanted her to be in pure ecstasy, I wanted Carmen all for myself, fuck men. I stuck my fingers in her sweetness to feel the warmth of her pussy. Goddamn! She was wet as hell.

"Baby, that feels fucking good…" she moaned.

I pulled my fingers out and made her taste them. One by one she sucked on my fingers like a blow pop. I couldn't wait to taste her and make that love come down. I was feeling really confident like I was a pro at this. Actually, I watched enough porn. That's the only reason why I knew what I was doing…

I worked my way down to her clit as she started to squirm. When I got to her butterfly I licked around it and worked my way down. Her pussy was so pretty I just wanted to stare at it.

"Ma this about to be the best head you ever got."

I stuck my tongue in Carmen's love tunnel and it tasted so sweet. I knew it would be good, it tasted like peaches. She yelled "Oh my God" as the feelings rushed over her. I licked around her clit moving my tongue in and out until I started to suck on it. As I sucked harder and harder I knew I had her. I couldn't wait to stick my strap on in her and fuck the shit out of her. I was determined that night. This shit was turning me on so much my sweetness was on fire. Right before she was about to let it out I stopped. I made her lick my breasts with her tongue ring. "Baby, why did you stop?" She asked panting and yearning for that nut. "Don't worry ma I got this, have you ever licked anyone's pussy before?" "No. I only kissed till now."

"Tonight you are going to taste me."

I stood and she got on her knees. I pushed her head into my pussy as she started to lick it.

"Carmen, lick that shit hard. I can't wait to fuck you."

Carmen's tongue felt so good, her tongue ring on my pussy felt like heaven. "Harder bitch! I want to cum in your mouth."

The devil got in me because I wanted her like I never wanted anyone in my life. Carmen sucked me like she did this before.

"Bitch, I said did you eat anyone's pussy before?"

"No baby, no…"

"Is this my pussy?" I said like a dude would say if he had a dick in a bitch.

"Yes Mami, this is your pussy."

With that, I creamed all in her mouth and she sucked every drop of it.

I pulled her ponytail and looked in her eyes as they were dripping with lust. "That tasted so good Mami."

"I know it did bitch. Lie on the floor. I'm gonna finish what you started."

She did exactly what I said. I stuck my tongue directly into her with such force I knew she would erupt in minutes. I began fingering her as I sucked on her sweetness just waiting to take all of her love juice into my mouth.

Two minutes later she exploded. It all came, came tumbling down and I sucked it up, every last drop of it.

Fuck that was better than I imagined, I was thinking.

"Fuck me baby, fuck me with your hand. I need some dick." She said.

"I got better than a hand. I gotta dick."

I went to get my strap-on.

We went into the living room.

"Tell me how you want it bitch!" I asked dominating.

"I want it from the back nice and hard."

I turned her around on the couch with her ass facing me. I got behind her and slid my dick in her. I felt so powerful at that moment, the feeling was invigorating. I had ten long inches in her and she was taking all of me like a champ.

That pussy was mine no way she would want a man after this.

We moved to the floor where she got on her knees, doggy style.

"You like this dick?"

"Hell yea, I love it!"

She was making her ass clap for me as I was riding her from the back, it was so erotic. Just at that moment she squirted all over the place.

"Mami, I love you!" She yelled as we both collapsed onto the floor.

"I'm yours baby, forever" Carmen whispered in my ear.

I knew she was mine. It doesn't get any better.

Central Park Sex

Monica Martinez

One Saturday afternoon they met and decided to take a walk through Central Park. Victor and Sheila were holding hands enjoying the sights. Victor teased Sheila with playful flirts. He leaned over and kissed her softly on the lips. Sheila felt as if electricity went through her entire body. He always made her feel like she would do things to him she never could imagine. They came across this rock that was in the middle of a path. Sheila took her shoes off.

She turned to Victor and said, "Let's go to the top of the rock."

They climbed the rock. Victor sat at first then put his

back to the rock to get some sun. She rested on his chest.

She reached to kiss his full lips. She bit his lower lip softly sucking on it. His hand began to caress her lovely breasts. He made her nipples erect through the dress. This man made her want to explore him. His hand started to work its way down her dress and went straight for her cherry. He realized Sheila was wet and joking he said, "Let's fuck right here."

Never in a million years would she have dreamed of doing such a thing. Sheila was hot and nervous all at the same time. There were people around them walking. She thought someone might see them but still someone might…

She straddled him pretending to be playing around with him. His dick was standing to attention. He was ready.

"Oh word?" He said. "It's on."

He unzipped his pants and let his dick free. Since she had on a dress it covered them, preventing others view of what was really going on. She rotated her hips on his hard cock. At first slow movements as she watched the people below walking by them. The thought of someone seeing them made Sheila more aroused. She arched her back taking his pipe deep inside of her canal. She moaned quietly because of the people walking around them. He reached for her breasts and took them in his hands as he helped with her movements. His hands went underneath her dress caressing her thighs and grabbing at her ass.

He playfully smacked her ass. Her strokes on him became more intense. She moaned and climaxed onto his pipe. As her cream dripped onto his manhood he took his fingers to collect it. He brought his fingers to her lips. Sheila sucked on them one by one enjoying the taste. Victor enjoyed the fact they were actually fucking in public. His dick got harder. His strokes were with much more force than before. He pinched her nipples so hard through her dress she almost yelled out. Instead he covered her mouth with his hand. Sheila felt the rush of hot cum hitting her walls. It felt hot as her pussy contracted not ready to let him go. The wind softly blew across her face and it felt amazing as she opened her eyes remembering they were outside.

This had been the most daring thing she had ever done in her life. Sheila gave him a couple more strokes and a chance to put his now soft dick back into his pants before climbing off of him. They stayed on the rock for another hour or so just basking in the sun. When they left the park the two of them couldn't stop smiling at each other.

Threesome

Monica Martinez

Tyrese took his girlfriend Lilliana to Esculita, a club on 38th Street and 8th Avenue. The club was visited mostly by bi-sexual women on Friday nights. Lilliana wanted to go, kept on pestering him until he finally took her. They were having a good time, enjoying each other's company and dancing.

The DJ started spinning; I Get so High by Toni Braxton. Lilliana loved that song because it refers to women who masturbate. Lilliana made her way to the empty dance floor to put on a show for Tyrese. He stayed at the bar, watching her. She started to move her body like a belly dancer. Her hair fell to her face. She pushed it away to make eye contact with Tyrese. She sang along with the words of the song as she danced.

Tyrese didn't take his eyes away. He was enjoying his girlfriend's performance till he couldn't take it anymore. He had to join her. He left the bar, joining her on the dance floor. Lilliana took her hands and ran them down the front of her body while moving to the beat of the song. She gyrated her hips like she were actually grinding on his manhood. She dropped low to the floor and moved back up with one of her hands touching her pussy. Lilliana's nipples were erect. He could see that through the sheerness of the dress she wore. She closed her eyes, for a moment she was gone with thoughts about sexing Tyrese. She thought about the yet to come sex they would have later on that night.

When the song finished Tyrese said, "Damn baby that was hot."

She whispered, "That's not all I have in store for you tonight."

Back at the bar, they ordered some more drinks enjoying each other's company and the ambiance of the club. They started to play truth or dare. Lilliana took a dare.

Tyrese dared her to hit on a chick in the club.

Lilliana looked at him and said "Bet."

She went to find a suitable victim. Lilliana wasn't the sort of broad who backed away from a dare. She figured she would show him how daring she was. Lilliana walked over to the other end of the bar. There was a beautiful young lady standing by herself. Lilliana offered to buy her a drink. The women accepted. Soon the two were small talking. Tyrese was amazed at how easy Lilliana made things, but they were in the club on bi-sexual Fridays.

The two women hit it off immediately. After the young lady finished her drink, Lilliana took her to the dance floor. They started dancing to Chris Brown's, Take You Down, as Tyrese watched them from the bar. The victim's name was Sonia. Lilliana had Sonia facing Tyrese as she danced behind her. She put her hands on Sonia hips. Sonia moved her arms to reach over Lilliana's neck as they danced.

Lilliana whispered in Sonia's ear, "I find you so damn sexy."

Sonia turned her head to Lilliana, "Ditto."

The two women started to kiss each other. Lilliana looked to see Tyrese's facial expressions.

His eyes were silver dollar wide. Lilliana saw his lips utter 'damn'.

Lilliana smiled. Tyrese couldn't believe she actually managed to pull a woman that damn quick. Lilliana started to grind onto Sonia.

Tyrese was getting aroused. He sat straight in his chair. Lilliana told Sonia about Tyrese. Sonia waved to him in response. Tyrese asked himself if this was really happening. It was right in front of his eyes.

The women made their way off the dance floor. They went to the bar, where Tyrese was. Lilliana introduced her new found friend to him.

Lilliana leaned over and whispered in his ear, "Papi I'm wet. I'm going to make this a night you'll never forget."

Tyrese grinned.

The trio stayed at the club dancing and drinking for another two hours. Lilliana was horny by the time they were ready to leave. Once they exited the club Lilliana grabbed Sonia's hand before she could walk anywhere. "Would you like to come with us?" She asked Sonia.

She told her victim that they had a hotel room in the city.

After a bit of speculating Sonia agreed to join them.

Lilliana and Tyrese couldn't wait to play with her. They entered the hotel room. Sonia and Lilliana couldn't keep their hands off of each other. After some time, the two women notice Tyrese's manhood was standing at attention through his jeans.

Tyrese grabs at his hardened bulge and told them, "I want the both of you."

The two women begin kissing. Tyrese walked behind Lillian and started to caress her. He took Lilliana's dress off. He got on his knees and took her dripping pussy into his mouth. Lilliana moaned. Sonia sucked on Lilliana's breasts. Lilliana started to go crazy. They tasted her at once and it was making her hotter.

Eventually, Lilliana said, "Have a seat." to Tyrese.

She wanted him to watch for a little while. He did what she wanted. Once that was settled she undressed the victim...

Lilliana took Sonia's breast in her mouth, sucking them one at a time while looking directly at Tyrese. Tyrese's dick was hard to the point it began to hurt from the pulsating. He began to stroke his rod as Lilliana played with her new found toy. Lilliana backed Sonia to the bed and pushed her to the mattress. Then she explored her body.

She gave Sonia soft kisses on her neck working her way

down. Tyrese was moaning, he was excited. He was enjoying the show. Lilliana was at Sonia's breast licking and teasing her. Tyrese stood for a better view. Lilliana took her tits her mouth with such tenderness. Tyrese tried to get closer. Lilliana shook her head, no. All he could do was watch.

Sonia crooned with delight enjoying Lillian's tongue skills. Lilliana moved her fingers down to Sonia's sweetness, she was wet. Lillian inserted a finger into Sonia took it out and brought it to her mouth. She needed to taste her. Lilliana craved more of Sonia. She went completely atop Sonia, licking from her breasts down to her sweetness. She took Sonia's sweetness into her mouth; Lilliana's sweetness was facing Tyrese. He saw it dripping with juices from being excited. He wanted to touch her. He crept closer, sneakily stuck a finger inside of Lilliana's pussy. Since she didn't object he took her pussy into his mouth. Lilliana lifted Sonia's legs to get closer to her pussy, wanting to taste her completely. Sonia began to pant and beg for Lilliana not to stop. Sonia released her juices into Lilliana's mouth. Her body was trembling with pleasure.

Lilliana motioned for Tyrese to join in the fray completely. He immediately got from his girlfriend and rushed to Sonia. He began to suck on Sonia's nipples. Sonia went crazy with the two of them working on her. Tyrese's dick was throbbing. Lilliana was still eating Sonia, tasting her juices and fingering her. Sonia reached for Tyrese's dick and placed it in her mouth. Tyrese let out a loud grunt it felt good. Lilliana took notice to Tyrese more. Both women started to share Tyrese's dick. Pushing him deep into their mouths, they began taking turns sucking and, licking it. Tyrese put his hands on both of their heads. He enjoyed the feelings they were giving him. He told both of the women to turn around so their backsides were facing him. He got on his knees to taste them one at a time.

The women were feeling good. They began kissing while he made them cum into his mouth. Tyrese sat back on the chair. Lilliana climbed to his mouth and Sonia climbed onto his erection. Sonia was riding him while Lilliana grinded on his mouth. The two women were facing each other while they shared a kiss. Tyrese couldn't hold it anymore.

He screamed. "I'm going to fucking cum."

Sonia jumped off of his dick. Lilliana moved away from his mouth. They both got on their knees, and opened their mouths to take his hot cum.

They shared a kiss with his hot cum in their mouths, playing with each other. Lillian brought Sonia to another orgasm with her fingers. Sonia screamed and her body shivered with pleasure. Lilliana sucked on Sonia's clitoris, while Tyrese was taking her to pleasure.

Lilliana was going to release any moment. Tyrese knew it. Tyrese wanted Sonia to take Lilliana's juices in her mouth. He grabbed Sonia's head and put it close to Lilliana's pussy. Without any hesitation Sonia took Lilliana's juices into her mouth. Lilliana grabbed onto Tyrese. She released inside of Sonia's mouth screaming…

The three of them were on the bed for a while relishing. They knew it was just the beginning of the night…

Erotic Story
Monica Martinez

Efrain and I have been married for seven years and our sex life has always been good. I continue to think of new ways to entice him and keep it fresh. As a suggestion, one of my girlfriends told me about an erotic book I should read to him. I thought it was a good idea because we had never done this before.

I went to Barnes and Nobles and picked up a copy of a book with erotic encounters. I read a few pages wanting to make sure it was good material before reading them to Efrain. Once I got home I began cooking dinner. While the food was on the stove I jumped into the shower. Efrain would get home at his usual time, seven, and we would sit with our two children and have dinner. After dinner, I finished cleaning the kitchen and told my two boys to take their bath. Like always I read them a story and kissed them goodnight.

It was now mine and Efrain's alone time. Efrain was in the shower when I entered our bedroom. *Great* I thought as I grabbed the teddy I purchased from Victoria's Secret. I was in the bed waiting for him to finish. He came into our bedroom smiling.

Damn after all these years I find him as sexy as I first did. He has gained weight since we got married. However, my Daddy is still sexy. He stands 5'9 170 lbs, nice big arms, has a little belly but not much though. His eyes are gray and he has dark brown hair with a little grey on the sides. His skin is cream.

I said to him, "Lay down, I want to read something to you."

I began to read him a story about a woman who masturbates to porn. He was wowed by the tale. He began to get aroused.

"Monique I got something for you" His dick was getting hard and rising out the top of his underwear. He grabbed my hand, leading it to his hardness. He said. "I want to fuck."

I moved towards him and tongued him down. As we shared the heated kiss, my pussy was throbbing and nectar began to seep out. I started to suck on his neck, worked my way down to the prize. He was grunting and panting as I got to the tip of his member. I began to lick it like it was a green apple blow pop. I licked around the tip back to the top. I inserted my tongue into his little slit, teasing his dick. Efrain grabbed my head and thrust his cock deep into my mouth. I bobbed my head up and down as my saliva ran down his shaft. He was as aroused as he could get. He pushed my head off of his dick.

We got into sixty-nine position. I continued to suck on his hardness as he sucked my pussy, teasing my clit. Efrain moved his tongue up and down my fat pussy. He stopped. We switched to another position. Now he had me on all fours with my face down into the pillow. He came around the bed, started to play and tease my 'tulip' with his fingers. I was soaked; he moved his hand to my hidden quarter pleasure. He lubricated it by spitting directly into the crack. This turned me on in ways I could only dream of. I couldn't contain myself and grinded my 'flower' hard against his mouth. I demanded for him to bring me to ecstasy. I came immediately as he inserted his eight inch rod inside of me.

Efrain was still fingering my hidden quarter as my pussy contracted on his rod. I began to bounce my ass up and down onto his finger. I was ready to explode and yelled "Daddy I'm gonna cum." He pulled his finger out of my ass. He grabbed my neck with a soft tug. I remember coming so hard from both places. It made me feel so dizzy. My body trembled with pleasure as yet another double orgasm came. Efrain's dick was pulsating inside of my wet walls. He was gonna try to release soon...

I started to tighten my pussy muscles onto his dick not letting him go and moving my body with his. He continued to strum me with long hard strokes. He took his rod out from my wetness releasing onto my backside...

He fell to the bed and said, "Damn I love our sex life, it's unbelievable."

I couldn't help but smile. I told him. "I love it more."

The two of us decided to shower and enjoy ourselves again. Once is surely not enough for this evening...

Staircase
Monica Martinez

Edwin and I came from a club this particular night. I was hot and bothered as we entered our house. I grabbed at his manhood and started to kiss him while going up the stairs. I was facing backwards. He was facing me. I stopped at the top of the staircase.

"I want you to fuck me right here, on the stairs."

He was so excited because he had never heard me say such a thing or seen me this way before. I pulled at his clothes trying to rip them off. He saw the devilish look in my eyes. He took my skirt off. He lowered himself down and gently kissed my sweetness. My juices were cascading down heavy. He left my panties on, moving to my bra. He removed it. He started to lick around my nipples making them erect.

My head was leaned against the stair. I was enjoying what he was giving me. I started to rub on my clit while he had my breast in his mouth. I took my fingers inserted them into my sweetness. My fingers collected my juice. I brought them to his mouth. He sucked on my fingers as I sucked on his neck. I kissed him so we both could taste my essence. It was sweet and mouth-watering. He continued to get excited. He lifted one of my legs and brought his head down to my sweetness all the while kissing my inner thighs. I was so excited I wanted to feel him enter me already.

I yelled, "Fuck me, fuck me right here Daddy."

He told me he wasn't ready to enter me. He proceeded to lick on the outside of my panties. He moved my panties to the side and started to pull on my outer lips with his lips.

Fuck this I said to myself. I started to rub my 'baby girl' into his mouth. I held onto his head saying, "Yeah Edwin, just like that." I wanted to cum in his mouth so I grinded harder. I began to pant and screamed, "Take that pussy in your mouth Papi. You like eating on this hot pussy?"

He got completely aroused as he started to move his tongue faster and deeper into me. I couldn't hold it any longer. I released into his mouth breathing heavily and feeling so tired afterwards. He took it all in his mouth placing two of his fingers into my sweetness. He fingered fucked me, while he pulled his hard dick out of his pants. He lifted my head from the stairs and put his cock into my mouth. There was pre-cum on it. I sucked it off the tip of his dick with a gulp.

I looked dead in his eyes and ask him, "You want me to suck this fucking cock?"

Of course he said, yes.

I took his cock deep inside my warm mouth without any hesitation. He let out a grunt.

"Yeah baby, suck that fucking cock."

I bobbed my head up and down his shaft like a porn star while he was finger fucking me keeping 'baby girl' moist. I was throbbing for his dick to be inside of me, licking his shaft as if it was a candy cane. I stroked his shaft hard as I continued sucking on him moving my head faster with each stroke. His eyes were closed. I knew he was feeling good. He was holding onto the staircase railing as his body started to shake.

I stopped, looked to him. "I want you to cum so deep down in my throat."

This excited him even more. He grabbed my head with

both hands and started to fuck my mouth with a little extra force.

He yelled, "Take that fucking cock."

I took it all, kept the saliva from drooling out my mouth. He was talking dirty, telling me how much he loves when I suck on his cock. He likes to call me his slut when I make him this hot. He moved faster thrusting into my mouth. It was so exciting to watch this man lose control. I worked his manhood contracting on it tighter. I felt him throbbing and growing. I felt him erupting into my mouth. It shot to the back of my throat filling my mouth. When I could speak, I told him I loved it.

He quickly lifted me into doggie style position. He entered me and began fucking me. He pushed deep inside of me giving me all of him. It hurt but it was a good hurt. I started to bounce my ass onto his dick begging for him to give me more.

"Harder." I screamed.

Harder he went.

"Deeper." I screamed.

Deeper he went.

He lifted to get deeper inside of me. He was pumping and giving me the feelings of pleasure unknown to any woman. His dick is strong and big. *Jeez this feels good,* is all I can think. He put my leg down and told me to hold onto one of the stairs. I did as he requested. He went up and down deeper inside my sweetness. He was circling around, I felt him all over my walls. He grabbed my breasts into his hands while he was fucking me pulling on my nipples. I lifted my head and turned to kiss him.

I yelled to him. "I'm about to explode."

He moved faster pulling on my hair.

He yelled at me, "Whose pussy is this?"

I whimpered back, "It's yours; It's all yours."

"Take my fucking cock you little slut." He yelled.

"I'm going to cum" I told him screaming as my body started to shake.

He took his nature out of me and got on his knees. I squirted cum into his mouth. My body was trembling I felt weary. I fell back onto the stairs. He lifted me back up, kissing my back as he entered me again. Damn he wasn't quite done with me. He leaned me over I had to hold onto the banister. He started to fuck me harder than before.

I yelped.

"Talk dirty to me, my little slut."

I yelled, "Fuck me harder. Give me that hard cock. Fuck that slut; give it to me."

All I heard was him moaning and panting. He grabbed

my ass spreading it apart.

"Yeah," I said to him, "Just like that Daddy. Spit in it…"

This drove him crazy. He tiptoed and gave me his cock real deep. He spit in the crack of my ass and pulled it apart. Fuck, that shit aroused me. He bounced faster. He was sweating. I knew he was at his peak.

"Come big Daddy, cum in my mouth." I yelled.

He quickly turned me around, shot his cum in my wide open mouth and down my chest.

"Fuck baby, it was good."

We were both exhausted afterwards. We staggered to our bedroom. The night was over now.

Slick

Monica Martinez

Hot damn, he was fine. I remember him like it was yesterday. They called him Slick. He was tall and handsome, 6', and 165 lbs. His body was packing nothing but muscles. He was Puerto Rican and German with Jet black hair and intense blue eyes. His lips were full, just like Mick Jagger's. He had high cheek bones, a straight nose, and a dark olive complexion. He defined fine. I'd seen him around the school cafeteria every now and then or in the hallway while I was heading to class. He never approached me. I would have given him my number without thinking twice. Word had it he was the biggest player in school. Honestly, I didn't care.

I wanted him to be mine. I was hot for him the moment I peeped him. I knew he was packing. And that just made me want him more.

Although I wanted him, I would never step to him. Mother taught us to let the guy come to us. Otherwise you were the girl to get a bad rep. I was not a virgin, but I wasn't a slut either. I had lost my virginity at seventeen, what a joke! I slept with him one time before I found out he was playing me. Well now Efrain was my ex and my eyes were on Slick. My friends warned me to stay away from him. Slick sparked my interest; there wasn't a doubt about it.

One day Slick stepped to me. He knew my name. I felt myself drip the instant it left his lips. He caught my ass walking to the train and asked if he could walk with me. The words, *'Marissa stay away from him'* immediately came to mind. I ignored the warning and allowed him to walk with me. He formally introduced himself with his government name.

"My name is Charles." He said in his deep seducing voice. I was thinking, *wow, you went from Slick to Charles...*

"How impressive," I told him.

We both chucked.

He wanted to know more about me. The questions were flying from his mouth. Funny, we had been going to the same school for years and never once said a single thing to one another. As we walked we talked like we'd done so for years. I thought it was fate. I was thrilled. We lived on opposite sides of the city. I reside in Bayridge Brooklyn, him in Corona Queens. I thought it was the beginning of something wonderful...

After we got acquainted Slick rode me home on the train for the rest of the week. He never asked me for my phone number. I was so frustrated I forgot all about my mother's words and yelled. "When are you going to ask for my number?"

He smiled. "I didn't know you wanted me to have it."

That was the beginning of us...

I hadn't told any of my girls we were kicking it. I figured they would find out eventually. It wasn't a secret we had been leaving the school together every day. We had a lot of things in common. It was a perfect fit in my eyes.

Slick was definitely a hottie. His blue eyes pierced through your body. Made you cum the instant he looked you over. His eyes could caress your body and make you feel as if you were the only women in the world. He had game; there was no doubt about it. No wonder they called him Slick. His words were smoother than your skin.

Two weeks later Slick convinced me it was time to play hooky with him. I totally disregarded the warnings I received about him. I took the train like any other day heading to school. Only I would be getting off at the Jackson Heights train station instead of 69th Street. I went to where he resided and called him from a payphone to let him know I was at the train station. He came to me in exactly five minutes.

He greeted me with such an intense kiss. I knew once I we were upstairs at his place, I was gonna give him anything he wanted. His kiss had sent a shiver straight to my kitty.

Soon we walked into Slick's place. I was nervous. I had only been with one guy before and I didn't know what to expect. I never really cut school before but there I was in Slick's apartment knowing that anything could happen. He led me straight to his bedroom. He told me he just wanted to show me where he slept. In my head I thought, *yeah aight he is really Slick.*

Upon entering the room I knew there was no turning back and shit was gonna pop off. I could feel the sexual tension.

He said, "Marissa, let's chill in here and watch some T.V."

We sat on his bed and then found ourselves laying on it. I must say for the first hour dude did nothing, to my surprise. He was playing chess making his moves at the appropriate time. I fell asleep on his chest watching T.V. while he was playing with my hair...

I awoke to his beautiful lips kissing me. He was caressing my body. Damn, it felt good to have his strong hands touch me. He was gentle. Within minutes I was kissing him back with lust he had awoken something deep within me. My kitty was pulsating, something I had never felt with Efrain. Before I knew it Slick had his hands on my jeans. He unzippered them and pulling them off. I didn't fight the feelings as he zeroed in on my panties. He took them off as well. He smiled at me. I said nothing. He moved to my sweetness and smelled it.

I had never been eaten out. I was bugging out when he was down by my 'girl'. He gently pulled my second set of lips apart and stuck his tongue into my pussy. I didn't know how to react, but it felt damn good. He asked if I liked it. I shook my head, yes.

He asked, "Have you ever had your pussy eaten out?"

I couldn't answer with words. I shook my head in a no motion.

Slick slid his tongue deep into my pussy. I gasped for

air. He licked my pussy from top to bottom and sucked on my clit. He was making me feel better then good. I moaned as he ate me out. He made me cum several times before he moved away from my sweetness. He got off the bed to take his pants off. His dick was big. Actually, it was the first time I got a good look at one. I had never looked at Efrain's full naked body because I was always worried about keeping the covers on me and not showing my body to him. However, here I was naked from the bottom down staring at a big dick. The girth on him was thick as well. I was pretty nervous as to how the heck he was gonna fit his dick inside of me.

Slick asked if I was okay.

I shook my head, said, "I'm nervous."

"No need to be nervous, you are safe with me. I want to make you happy and take care of you forever."

The words sounded so beautiful and genuine. All I could do was smile. He came to the bed and positioned himself on top of me, spreading my legs apart to get in between them. Slick grabbed my hand and made me touch his big dick. He asked for me to stroke it as we kissed. I did exactly what he wanted me to. My pussy was dripping. I was scared and excited at the same time.

He brushed my hand away, placed the tip of his dick into my pussy. He took his time pushing in, my pussy was tight, it didn't matter how dude had me excited. I began to get uncomfortable because it was hurting instead of feeling good. Slick pushed forward regardless. I cried. He held me close to him.

"Marissa, I love you, don't cry."

The words sounded sincere for the moment as he moved deeper inside of me I felt something break.

I cried again screaming his name, "Slick…!" I told him "You're hurting me."

He pulled his dick out and got off me. He looked down at my pussy. "Are you due for your period?"

I just had my period the week before, I thought.

"No, Why?" I asked.

He said, "You're bleeding."

I jumped from the bed and run to the bathroom. I didn't know what was going on. He followed behind me.

"Marissa, are you a virgin?"

I turned to him.

"Slick, I slept with one guy, my boyfriend of two years over eights months ago."

He asked if I bled with him. I didn't remember doing

so, matter of fact Efrain didn't stay in me very long. I remembered him cumming very quickly probably two minutes into our ordeal and it was over. Slick smiled at me.

"It's okay. It's not your period, come back to my room."

I followed him back to his room. He laid me down once again. He began to kiss me all over again and moved back down to my pussy. He ate me out again, and damn this time it felt so much better. After the eating, he moved towards my neck and sucked leaving a hickey there.

"Marissa, I love you. I'm gonna love you forever. You're going to be my wife."

My mind went into a different land bugging out, wondering if dude was out of his mind. We had only been kicking it for all of two weeks. How could he love me? He pushed his dick to the tip of my pussy again and told me it would only hurt for a minute because he was really taking my virginity. Efrain hadn't sexed me right he said.

True to his word it hurt for only a minute before his nine inch dick was filling my sweetness and making me cream beyond belief. With each stroke of his dick my body loosened and I wanted more.

I began scratching his back as he whispered how much he loved me. I never once said the words back because at that moment I thought it was game he was giving me. We made love the rest of the day. Each time it was better then the first. Slick had me. I knew I was gonna be hooked. I just didn't know how long it was gonna to be. I didn't know if he was just saying the words 'I love you' because he was getting the pussy. I knew actions would speak louder then words. If the next day came and dude didn't look for me, then he was really '*Slick*' all along.

At 2:30 we finished. I showered and headed home. He took me to the train station. Once there he kissed me.

"Marissa, I meant everything I said to you upstairs" He said as he looked me in my eyes.

I smiled. "Slick, I gotta get going, otherwise, my mom's is gonna know I played hooky."

I jumped on the train and headed back to Brooklyn with a huge smile on my face. This time I had lost my virginity to someone who really loved me, so I thought?

Slick was true to the word around the school. We continued to kick it. I was officially his girl and everyone knew it. The other chicks in school didn't respect it though. They continued to throw pussy at Slick and he was '*Slick*' in every sense of the word. Dude claimed to love me yet he played me several times through-out our so called relationship. Only I didn't know how to let go because dude had me hooked.

Dulce de Leche

Monica Martinez

Frank and I have been together for ten years now. I must say every day I find him more attracted than the day before and I love him more each and every day. He has loved me unconditionally and has let me explore my sexual desires without passing judgment on me. I am grateful every day the man above has blessed me with such a beautiful man. Our commitment to each other is very rare especially in the Latino Community. Most of our men are Machismo. Frank however doesn't mind my independence.

We met sixteen years ago in Manhattan it was kind of

funny actually. He was driving a truck delivering to the Water Club on 30th street and 1st Avenue. My girlfriend and I were headed out to lunch. We stepped off the curb like every other New Yorker does when we don't have the light thinking somehow we could get across regardless of the traffic.

Frank drove his truck right to the corner where Dannie and I were, we had to jump back onto the sidewalk. Once the light changed we started to walk and I wanted to see who the hell was in the truck that was trying to run us over and to my surprise was the most handsome man I had ever seen.

His eyes were hazel and his skin the color of cream. He had his hair pushed back and his features were lovely. His chiseled face with define features. His lips full and I was stuck on dumb mode. Dannie pushed me forward and said Monica keep moving. As I did he waved at me and I waved back with a smile, inviting him to come for more.

He caught me off guard and I turned around and he said "Hey my name is Frank and I can't talk long because I left my truck running but I wanted to give you my card with my number. I would love to take you out if possible." With that he ran back to his truck and I looked at my girlfriend and smiled.

Frank and I started off as friends with innocent dinners and lunches. We gradually worked our way to our current status. I didn't make love to him until two years of knowing him. The longer you wait to have sex proves how much of a good girl you really are. Well that's what I was taught as a young girl.

The first time we made love I couldn't believe the intensity and the passion we shared. He made love to me like no other. I actually saw stars as I came to an orgasm, one of many he provided to me back then.

Although we didn't get into a committed relationship till ten years ago. Fourteen years later I still can't believe the heights he continues to take me too. We make love daily and sometimes twice or three times a day. He has shown my body the true meaning of Dulce de Leche.

The sweet milk pours out from my sweetness the moment he is there licking, sucking on my clit. The flicker of his tongue makes me gush instantly. He drinks my sweet milk at any given time she pours out onto his tongue. It's breathtaking almost an art for him, because he is truly wonderful at it.

He makes love to me like it's the first time over and over again. We still share the same hunger for each other from the first moment we made love. His strong long hands caress my body with tenderness yet firmness indicating he is still attracted to me.

One should only experience true love such as we found with each other.

Kiss Goodnight: *Damyico R.*

Lips meet lips
But one set don't speak
Only moisten in anticipation
Of pleasure to cum, hip flexes to receive
as tongue parts lips, and circles her tongue
but just with the tip, she moans uncontrollably
but this is only the beginning
intrigued by her response, my tongue
explores deeper rapid waves of pleasure
sending chills, up and down her spine
hands reaching for object
but hands only grasp air
eyes begin to roll
legs tighten around my neck
toes curled like two fist
minutes of intensity mouths open
but she can hardly speak
simply cries of yes
as her bodies at release
mmm… tasty
now back to sleep
just wanted to
kiss you goodnight

GLOSSARY

Dulce De Leche:	Sweet Milk
Hola:	Hello
Chulo:	Handsome
Dame mas:	Give me more
Te amo:	I love you
Que Rico:	Feels good
Dame eso:	Give it to me
Cono:	Damn
Diablo:	Devil
Aye dios mios:	Oh my God
Hazme el amor:	Make Love to me
Aye:	Oh
Si:	Yes
Papi:	Daddy
Carjo:	Shit
Hay Puenta	Shit
Nena	Girl
Me Gusta	I like
Mi Amor	My Love

ABOUT THE AUTHOR

$\mathcal{M}$onica S. Martinez was born and raised in Queens, NY, she started to write poetry at the age of twelve, and later experimented with song writing. In 2004 Monica opened an in-home party business promoting adult novelties. With the premise of providing women educational information to help keep their relationships alive, spicy and fun, through her business Tantalizing Productions, Inc. she was invited into the lives and experiences of many clients. Hearing numerous stories which ranged from sexy, hot to just downright funny, she was lead back to her writing passion. After absorbing the information and a few ideas of her own, came the birth of ***Tantalizing Erotic Thoughts & Encounters,*** a series of short stories that will take you on a journey of discovery.

In 2007, three of her short stories were published in POSH, a Caribbean Entertainment & Lifestyle magazine.

Monica has been compared to other successful authors with a Latin twist yet she remains true to her urban roots. Continue to watch her as she writes urban drama which will take you to new heights and filled with mind blowing sex. Everyone will be able to relate on some level.

Monica still lives in New York with her family.

So enjoy the ride only if you dare to lose your inhibitions!

Please be sure to visit Monica's website for upcoming events, book signings and the release of the latest blog.

www.monicamartinez.org

Also, look out for upcoming Tantalizing Author Chante D. Graham.

www.chantegraham.com

COMING SOON!

Tangled Web

Charlene Rodriguez, hard working, independent Latina who has a stable relationship but unexpectedly falls for a complete stranger. Does love at first sight really exist? Does she say with the man whom she's currently seeing or will she venture out to follow her heart?

David Hernandez, madly in love with his girlfriend, frustrated because they haven't reached the next level in their relationship. In a weak moment, he has a lustful night of passion. Will he be able to hide it behind lies before it catches up to him?

Christina Williams, just landed a new job and is at the top of her game. The only thing she wants now is to settle down and finally have a family, after all her biological clock is ticking. To what extent will she go to fulfill these goals?

Maria Rodriguez, is faced with lies, deceit, and betrayal from the man she loves. As she moves forward things seem to rapidly spiral out of control. Will she be able to save herself and pick up the pieces of her broken life?

Antonio Rosario, a true player, in every sense of the word. He knows how to play the game while still being true to himself. He works hard, parties hard and has women at this beckon call. He feels he's on top of the world but is he really?

This story is based in Queens, New York around three couples who become intertwined in a web of love, lies and lust. It brings to light the popular saying "it's a small world after all" and open the doors to those who have felt the manipulation which love can bring. When it comes to love can anyone or anything be trusted?

Love, hate, lust, passion, loyalty, betrayal is a Tangled Web.